Date due

April 20

SCHAUMBURG TOWNSHIP DISTRICT LIBRARY

Please do not deface this card.
Please leave card as placed in book for correct due date.

50¢ fine if card is lost.

the LIES About Truth

Also by Courtney C. Stevens
Faking Normal

the LIES About Truth

Courtney C. Stevens

HARPER TEEN
An Imprint of HarperCollinsPublishers

HarperTeen is an imprint of HarperCollins Publishers.

The Lies About Truth
Copyright © 2015 by Courtney C. Stevens
All rights reserved. Printed in the United States of America.
No part of this book may be used or reproduced in any manner whatsoever
without written permission except in the case of brief quotations embodied
in critical articles and reviews. For information address HarperCollins
Children's Books, a division of HarperCollins Publishers, 195 Broadway,
New York, NY 10007.
www.epicreads.com

Library of Congress Cataloging-in-Publication Data
Stevens, Courtney C.
    The lies about truth / Courtney C. Stevens. — First edition.
        pages   cm
    Summary: "A teen struggles to overcome both the physical and
emotional scars that resulted from an accident that killed her best friend"—
Provided by publisher.
    ISBN 978-0-06-224541-0 (hardcover)
    [1. Friendship—Fiction.   2. Emotional problems—Fiction.
3. Forgiveness—Fiction.]   I. Title.
PZ7.S84384Li 2015   2014047815
[Fic]—dc23   CIP
                                                                 AC

Typography by Andrea Vandergrift
15 16 17 18 19   CG/RRDH   10 9 8 7 6 5 4 3 2 1

First Edition

To those with physical and emotional scars;
to those who feel sorry for the things they can't change;
to those broken ones who possess a gentle strength;
to those who do the right thing in the wrong way:
your humanity is beautiful.
Isaiah 61:3.

CHAPTER ONE

Night was like Christmas. There wasn't nearly enough of it to go around, especially in June. At 8:55, I walked down our little bayside street, crossed the road, and wound through the lot of the Worthy Wayfarer toward what I hoped was an empty shore. My company consisted of sand, circular thoughts, and a wretched pair of shorts.

Fletcher, my therapist, thought getting me back in clothes that didn't cover my whole body, even at night, was a step in the right direction. I'd agreed to try, and this was my first attempt at bare legs. It was dark, I was in my favorite place on the planet, and I was fine. Showing scars to no one *was fine.* That's what I told myself as I reached the dune walk.

I loved the abandoned beach. Loved the sound of sloshing tide. Loved when the Florida sand was neither hot nor cold, but perfectly warm between my painted toes. Over the last year, I'd forgotten the glorious *swish-swish* sound athletic fabric made during a run. That was the one thing about Fletcher's challenge I was looking forward to. Six miles of *swish-swish*. I pressed pause on my playlist and listened deeply: gulf breeze, ocean, my heartbeat, *swish-swish*, and . . . dang it.

There were people on *my* beach.

Ducking into the sea grass, I watched the scene—a graduation party. I'd gotten an invite—a pity nod, I'm sure—and I'd deleted the message. The smoky smell of bonfire flames licking wood tempted me to join the party. But wearing shorts, with this many people around . . . I couldn't think of anything worse.

This was Gray and Trent's class get-together, not mine, but a few of my former classmates sat on towels. A group of seniors danced and lifted Solo cups and sang off-key verses. Others sat on driftwood logs talking and laughing. Graduation had been two nights ago, and they all seemed to be sucking the last of high school through a tiny straw.

Good for them.

The fire and moonlight made slipping through the dunes seem unlikely, but I needed to run. And I wanted to keep my word about the shorts. The moment I stepped out of the shadows to dart toward the empty coastline owned by the military, Gina yelled my name.

"Sadie." The wave that came with her greeting was shallow and tentative, but her smile was canyon-deep.

She was genuinely happy to see me. If only I could reciprocate.

I froze on the spot and waited, standing between two towering dunes. There was something about being with an old friend that brought back habits, good and bad. Even after eleven months of awkward interactions.

"Hey, Gina," I said when she was still a few steps away.

She wove her windblown mane into a tight knot as she approached, and I envied the casual way she put her cheekbones on display. "You got my text," she said. "I hoped you'd come, but I can't believe you're here."

I tugged on the edge of my shorts and pointed to my shoes. "Actually, I was out for a run."

She didn't comment on the shorts, but her gaze lingered on my thigh and a long triangular scar I called Pink Floyd.

"You could come say hi," she suggested.

I backed away a few steps. "I don't think so."

Best friends, even former ones, were supposed to understand crap like social anxiety and scar exposure. All of my previous explanations had failed to register—or Gina couldn't accept that sometimes when things changed, they didn't change back. Even if we both wanted them to.

Gina's response was to rocket-launch me into another lion's den. "Um . . . Gray's here. I know he'd love to see you."

Every time we were together, she tried to sell me the same story. I didn't know whether it was supposed to lessen her guilt or increase mine for avoiding him.

"Please stop trying to fix—"

"I'm just saying you should hear him out. He's still not over you." Gina toed the sand and made a concerted effort to lift her eyes to mine. "Six years is a lot to throw away."

Gray Garrison and I were once comasters of the swings, sworn Potterheads, fellow indie band enthusiasts, and in some variation of young love, cooties and all, for every minute we'd known each other. A year ago, the high school halls had felt like a really long wedding aisle. A lot can change in a year.

"I'm sort of with Max," I told her.

Yes, Max was in another country, and yes, *with* was a relationship of emails, but we were our version of together. And maybe if I admitted that now, she'd stop pushing Gray at me.

Gina's pretty, scarless face—whose only technical imperfection was a smattering of adorable freckles—froze in surprise. "Um, that's great, Sadie." She shoved her hands into her pockets and shifted her weight back and forth before adding, "I just want to remind you there's *nothing*, still nothing, between me and Gray."

Except that one little bit of sex or something I'd interrupted.

"Not that it makes it okay, but we were all pretty messed up back then."

Back then wasn't that long ago.

"Neither of us ever meant"—she held up empty hands and gestured toward my face, toward the scar I called Idaho—"to hurt anyone."

I knew that.

Knowing something wasn't worth shit sometimes. This was exactly why I avoided talking to Gina. She always brought this up. Always told me she was so, so sorry. Always shoved me toward the past. And here we were back on that same treadmill.

The thing was, I believed her. Gray, too, for that matter. Neither made idle apologies or hurt people, especially me, intentionally. But they had, and I still couldn't muster up an *It's no big deal.* Or even an *It's a huge deal and I can't forgive you.* So she went on apologizing, and I went on keeping grudges.

Thank God for home school. At least I hadn't heard this every day.

Gina continued her babble. "Wouldn't it be nice to hang out again? You could walk over there with me, sit down, have a drink, ignore Gray if you want, tell me about running or surgeries or how Max is or . . . anything. I . . . miss you."

I missed her, too. The words wouldn't come out. I was immediately glad they hadn't, because Gray's hands landed on my shoulders, soft and gentle, interrupting everything. I knew they were his without spinning around. Body movements were like fingerprints; they were all unique. His was a choreography I used to dance to.

"Hey, you," he said.

How did a voice hovering over an ear have that much power?

"Hey, you," I said, and turned to face him.

Gray, with his boyish face and perfectly kissable nose. No

scars, no imperfections, except a right ear the tiniest bit lower than the left. He spread out his arms—a clear invitation—and out of either obligation or habit, I hugged him. His chin landed on top of my head, my face smooshed against his chest, his hands crisscrossed against my back.

Rubbing alcohol on open wounds hurt less.

One, we weren't a couple anymore. Two, once you've been held, you know what it feels like when there's no one to hold you. And three, he was Gray, both the guy and the color of this situation. Max and I emailed, but a computer couldn't whisper in my ear. A computer didn't have arms.

Gray let me go. "I'm glad you're out of the house," he said.

Not only was I out of the house, I was having a conversation with two—count them—people. Other than my parents, that didn't happen very often. I wasn't exactly scared of people, but people seemed scared of me.

"I was out for a run," I explained again, taking several steps back.

"Oh. I thought maybe . . ." His words trailed away, but the implication was clear. He thought I had come to see him or Gina. They'd both texted me about this party earlier in the week.

On a whim, I tested a theory. More to remind myself I was right than because I believed he'd changed.

I looked Gray straight in the eyes.

He looked away.

That didn't make him a monster, but it sure made me feel like one. Friendship, much less a relationship, was impossible when he couldn't stand the sight of me. So I was the one who had officially broken it off.

"Still can't do it," I said.

He knew what *it* meant, and sighed his regret. Gina reined us in, placing her hands on our shoulders. Always the peacemaker.

"I need to go," I said.

Before I sprinted away, Gina stopped me with a question. "Is Max coming back for the . . . anniversary?"

I nodded. If some people are knotted in friendship, we were all one big tangle. Gray and me. Gina and Trent. Max, Trent's tagalong little brother. Our foursome, occasionally fivesome, used to be inseparable. Neighbors, couples, and the second generation of friends in our families.

Our parents had stuck together over the past year.

We hadn't followed in their footsteps.

The wreck happened June 29. We were twenty-two days away from the one-year anniversary of Trent's death.

"I need to go," I said, more urgently than before.

"What about school?" she asked. "Are you coming back in the fall?"

I didn't want to talk about school or the anniversary. I wanted to run.

"Sorry. I gotta go," I said, in full retreat mode.

"I'll check in later," she said.

Gray just stood there sighing with his fingers laced behind his head. I'd heard him sigh more in the past year than in all the time we were a couple.

As I took off, my eyes drifted in the direction of the party. My old classmates were probably sighing too. Everyone out there knew about Trent, knew I'd gone through the window of his Yaris, knew why Gray and I broke up. They probably assumed I blamed Gina and Gray for more than cheating. (Fair assumption, as she was driving the car that caused my face to have a scar named Idaho. And he was right beside her.)

Maybe I did. Maybe I didn't. Blame was crazy complicated. Some days, everything—Trent's death, my face, all the break-ups, Max leaving the country—was Gina and Gray's fault. Some days, God was the fall guy. Some days, blame never entered my mind. I liked those days best. I didn't want to be an angry jerk who sat around reminiscing about old grievances and pointing fingers, but I couldn't seem to control the emotion with any accuracy.

All I knew was that the farther I got from the party, the more I wished Gina or Gray would come after me. Neither of them did, so I cranked up my music and ran. I wasn't a sprinter, and after a mile, my lungs reminded me of that.

I slowed to a stop, put my hands on my knees, and took a deep breath. In front of me, five concrete pylons rose out of the water like a broken-down gate. "The Wall," as we all called it, was once a military building on the shore. Now, thanks to a hurricane, it was a gull stoop at the one-mile mark. This was where I wrote my list in the sand.

Because it was damaged.

Because what it once was didn't matter to the birds.

Because I understood the Wall and the Wall understood me.

It was nice to have friendship with a place.

In the company of moonlight and Coldplay, I wrote the things I wanted from life this year.

1. Wear a tank top in public
2. Walk the line at graduation
3. Forgive Gina and Gray
4. Stop following. Start leading.
5. Drive a car again
6. Kiss someone without flinching
7. Visit the Fountain of Youth

Beneath the list, I scrawled the only Latin phrase I knew. *A posse ad esse.* It means . . . "from possibility to actuality."

Apart from the Fountain of Youth, these were simple, achievable things, in concept. Hell, some of them I could do in a day. But I'd had many days, many opportunities, many lists in the sand, and no progress. Nearly every night I wrote these things.

And every night the ocean washed them away.

Tonight—probably because I'd seen Gina and Gray, or maybe because I felt like that old broken-down wall—I added one thing beside number three.

And tell them the truth.

CHAPTER TWO

When I got home an hour later, I collapsed in the Adirondack chair on our back porch to catch my breath. Mom must have been listening for me. She opened the screen door before my butt hit the wood.

Leaning around the door, facing halfway inside and halfway out, she passed me a bottle of water and a business envelope. "Good run?" she asked.

"Yeah."

Her voice teetered between worried and pretending she wasn't worried. "You were gone for a while. Shorts okay?"

Shorts hadn't turned out to be the hard part of tonight.

"Yeah."

"Can I sit for minute?" she asked.

I patted the chair next to me, welcoming her company.

Mom tugged the door closed and sat down. In unison, we stared at the McCalls' house, as if we expected Trent or Max to emerge and head to the bay for some night fishing. At first, she stayed quiet, thinking. Then she said, "Dad and I talked about the home-school thing while you were out."

"And?" I asked, draining the bottle of water.

Mom had a habit of pinching her lips with her hand when she had to deliver bad news. She pinched five times. I braced myself.

"We don't think it's a good idea," she began. "We did it last year because of the surgeries and rehab, but this year . . ."

She'd hesitated lately when we'd talked about school, but she'd never come out and said she wouldn't do it.

I sat up, suddenly feeling nauseous.

"Mom," I said with as much protest as I could.

"Kiddo, you can't hide from people the rest of your life."

My shoulders sagged, but I found some energy to fight back. "Sure I can. There's a lovely disorder called agoraphobia—"

"Not funny."

"With a face like this, I need humor."

"Honey, you're never going to be ready. You just need to go for it."

While I agreed with her in theory, gumption wasn't my strongest trait these days. I gripped the arms of the chair and exhaled for her benefit. "It would be helpful if you'd try to understand, for like two seconds, that I'm happy where I am."

"Except you're not."

God, she had me there. I'd just written *Walk the graduation line* an hour ago. Part of me clearly wanted to return to Coast Memorial. Just like I'd wanted to walk into that party tonight as if nothing had happened. Wanted to take selfies with Gina and post them to Instagram. Wanted Gray to look me in the eyes again. Wanted . . . my old life.

"Look, I'm not in your shoes. I get that," Mom said. "None of this has been easy. But we're worried. You didn't attend Gray and Trent's graduation with us. You're practically a hermit. Running at night. Hanging out at the salvage yard. You don't talk to anyone." She paused. "Sadie, this house used to be a revolving door."

Trent didn't graduate. I spared her that comment and defended myself. "I email with Max. And . . . I saw Gina and Gray tonight."

It was her turn to sigh at my excuses. We were like rhyming lines of a poem, perfectly following each other's lead.

"I'm glad you have Max and that you talked to Gina and Gray tonight, but that's not what Dad and I are talking about. It's a bigger shift than emails and one conversation. Dr. Glasson says you're ready."

I didn't answer her, and I'm sure she realized I wouldn't. My silence wasn't a lack of trust.

Mom pressed a kiss against Idaho. "Think about it. It's easier when it's your decision."

"Nothing's easy, Mom."

"We'll get through," she said, her voice piping with possibility. "I believe in you, kiddo. Just like I always have."

God, I wished she were pocket-size. Her hope was infectious.

"Okay," I said.

Moms have a habit of hovering when they don't want to say anything else, but they don't want to leave the vicinity. I tucked the envelope she'd given me under my thigh, hoping my sweat wouldn't soak through the paper, and pointed at the door.

"You aren't going to open it?" she prodded.

"Not with you standing there."

She chose to tease me rather than be offended. "I only wanted to . . . check for anthrax. Can't be too careful these days."

"Good *night*, Mom."

She blew me a kiss. "Don't stay out here too late."

Thankfully, she left me in peace. When she stopped watching through the kitchen window, I slid my finger under the flap and ripped through the envelope as I read the front. My name was typed, but there was no address. Weird. Maybe it was a prank. Or a late birthday card. Gina or Gray might have dropped it off. They were the most likely candidates since I'd fallen off the radar of my other friends. Max sent a few real cards and a package at Christmas, but if he'd mailed this from El Salvador, it would have had stamps.

I removed a single piece of typing paper from the envelope.

As I unfolded it, I scooted my chair toward the bulb in the center of the porch, expecting to have trouble seeing the words. There was no trouble at all. In the middle of the page was a single typed sentence.

> I turned thirteen years old today and I went skinny-dipping with Trent McCall.

I dropped the sheet of paper and covered my mouth with my hand.

"Sweet Jesus."

I wrote that sentence four years ago. Four years ago on a scrap of notebook paper. On a scrap of notebook paper that I put inside Big. Big, who was three parts stuffed animal, one part journal, and all parts mine. No one had ever seen it before.

Someone clearly had.

CHAPTER THREE

Rage. (n.) that gut feeling of disgust when your parents interfere with your life.

I wasn't certain when Mom and Dad decided it was acceptable to go through my personal belongings, but we were about to have words.

"Mom!" I yelled as I entered the kitchen. And since she didn't do this alone, I put Dad on the hook too. "Dad!"

They clearly hadn't anticipated my anger, as they were lounging in the TV room watching their latest Netflix obsession. I wanted them at the kitchen table. I wanted an explanation. Yelling as much, I watched them enter the room and eye me as if I were a Bigfoot they needed to tranq. I flung the envelope down. "You had no right to do this."

Dad's head tilted to the side. He spoke in a calm but stern voice. "Sit. Down."

I sat. Once I was down, I threw the envelope across the table. Paper looks angry when it's thrown.

"Would you like to tell us what this is about in a civil—"

I civilly interrupted him. "This is about you going through my stuff."

"No. This is about you cooling your jets, young lady," Dad answered.

Not one time in the past year had we taken these tones. Mom and Dad had been patient, supportive partners in my surgeries, recovery, and therapy. On the whole, I had very few complaints. But going into my room, pilfering my personal thoughts, typing them out like this . . . No one would be okay with that invasion of privacy. No one.

"You want to tell us what's going on?" Dad began.

I pointed to the envelope. "That's what's going on."

Dad started to remove the page. It was about then that I realized my parents appeared utterly clueless. If I'd gotten this wrong, my dad was getting ready to read a sentence I'd have a hard time explaining.

"Wait a minute." I snatched the paper away and looked at Mom. "You gave this to me on the porch. Where did you get it?"

"From the mailbox."

"It was just in there?" I asked.

"It was just in there," she repeated.

Time to backpedal. "Somebody played a joke on me." I pasted on a fake smile. "I thought it was y'all. Family meeting over. Go back to *House of Cards*. I'm really sorry I raised my voice."

Mom stared at the envelope. Dad looked uncertain how to proceed. I saw him wondering what it was about the envelope that had caused me to unhinge.

"Would you like to talk about it?" Mom asked.

I shook my head. "No. I'm sorry. I thought . . . I just thought wrong."

After a moment of uncomfortable silence, Dad said, "Honey, is all this"—he waved at my emotions as if they were another person in the room—"about the anniversary?"

"Don't talk about Trent, Dad. Please, I . . ." My voice shook, but I kept the tears in check. I missed Trent like I missed the person I used to be.

Makeup covered parts of my scars, but nothing covered up grief. My dad saw it on me.

"Look, kiddo." He knocked his knuckles on the table. "You've got to buck up."

"Tony." My mom tried to stop him, but he ignored her.

"No, Tara," he warned my mom in the same stern voice he'd warned me in earlier. "She's got enough courage in her, and we're going to help her get it out. We've talked about this."

"Hello, I'm right here." I waved, annoyed.

Dad turned his attention back to me. "I'm not trying to be insensitive. Just the opposite. I'm worried about you. . . . We're worried about you. Mom said we shouldn't push you back into school, but this outburst, or whatever it is, is more proof you need to be around people. This summer . . . you're going to be around people."

My stomach dropped into my toes. My voice quivered. "You're going to make me, aren't you?"

Mom and Dad exchanged a glance. "Yes," they said together.

I got up from the table and quietly pushed in my chair. "You don't understand—"

"We do."

It was a solemn chorus, a firm decision.

Mom stood and walked toward me. Her arms folded around me, stroking my hair. Her heart pressed into mine. I felt it beating against me, fast and strong, afraid and confident. Heartbeats are a dichotomy. I left my hands at my side.

"This isn't a punishment," she said. "We almost lost you. We're not going to stand back and watch you lose yourself."

"I get it. I get it," I mumbled.

I broke the embrace and walked down the hallway to my bathroom. I stripped myself down to skin and scars and stepped into a cold shower.

I didn't understand that paper, but I understood my mom and dad. Understood that they wouldn't budge, and my screaming *And if I don't?* would only force them to lay down more consequences. But I wanted to argue. I wanted to fight some more, and I didn't know why. I wanted to be furious at them, but some part of my brain said they were probably right.

I wouldn't be making lists in the sand if they weren't.

When a bad habit became a rut, people noticed. Especially when that rut was the size of the Grand Canyon.

The shower calmed my muscles but not my emotions. I retreated to my room and eyeballed the traitor, Big.

The stuffed blue ostrich sat, floppy and worn, in the middle of my pillows. Just where I'd left him this morning. It wasn't exactly public knowledge that I'd removed much of Big's polyfill stuffing and replaced it with paper scraps of my random thoughts. Actually, it narrowed the whodunthisshit to Gina, Gray, Max, Fletcher, Metal Pete . . . Who else? There were maybe a couple of girls from school who had seen Big on an overnight trip, but surely none of those people had time for something like this.

Big was soft in my hands and crinkly to my ears as I squeeze-checked him. He sounded and felt full. Digging carefully into the hole, I removed the first scrap and read. Shame is a fast emotion; I felt it within the first five words I'd written just last week.

I will stop drawing baseball threads around my scars with a Sharpie. I will stop.

I hadn't stopped yet. Three nights ago, after a deflating doctor's visit—"No, we can't do more surgery right now"—I'd gone back to the habit.

Folding the paper into a tiny square, I placed it on my night-stand and removed another. This was a tedious process. The papers weren't uniform and the hole was small. Ideally, every-thing—memory, secret, or thought—went in and stayed in.

When I unfolded the next one, I laughed. It was much older.

> I have now watched every single episode of
> Buffy the Vampire Slayer. Twice.

God, why couldn't the sender have picked that one?

I didn't even remember writing that. It must have been a while ago; I've seen the series five times now. There was no telling all the crap I'd shoved into Big over the past five years. As I held him, I realized there was no way to know what was there and what was missing. No way to know if someone had read everything or just that one thing. Searching for the skinny-dipping slip and hoping to God that, somehow, some-one had seen it fall out and had returned it to me discreetly was the only choice I had.

Of course, if that were the case, they wouldn't have typed and delivered it like a cloak-and-dagger asshole.

Still, I wished for a simple answer.

Not everything I removed from Big required an in-depth read. I bypassed plenty on Trent, the wreck, Gina and Gray, funny memories, ridiculous theories, and a slightly embarrassing number of overdramatic thoughts about everything from my period to my parents. Forty-one tries later, I hit the jackpot.

> I turned thirteen years old today and I went skinny-dipping with Trent McCall.

I hadn't expected to find it. But there it was. Despite my worries over who and how and what, the memory itself made me laugh.

I stared at my window now—wishing for a *tap, tap, tap*.

The night I wrote about started when Trent raised my windowpane a little after midnight. It had been my birthday for three minutes. "Sadie May, come with me. I have a plan."

Trent was good with plans. I hopped down beside him rather than ask what it was. He always had bread crumbs in his voice, and I followed them like a fairy tale.

Sneaking out was a novelty we both enjoyed, and so far, we hadn't been caught. We biked the two miles to the end of Santa Rosa Boulevard, then the remaining few miles toward Destin. Traffic on 98 zipped by us, but Trent never slowed down. I kept my eyes on the pavement as he pulled into the public parking on our side of the Destin Bridge.

"What are we doing?" I asked as we chained our bikes to a sign.

"Smoking, drinking, and skinning."

"Excuse me?"

He tapped his backpack. "You're a teenager now. We have to make it real."

"We didn't make it real when you turned thirteen," I argued, but really, I was pretty damn excited for whatever came next.

"That's because you weren't thirteen yet."

We laughed at his logic and walked through the soft sand toward the water's edge. The west jetty stretched like a long rock finger into the Gulf, creating a semi-boundary between the bay, Destin Harbor, and the open ocean. The jetty, like most things at the beach, looked closer than it was. Piers and markers often tricked your eyes, but Trent and I had made this walk to fish and snorkel plenty of times. Lights from the bridge and a nearly full moon accented the water with golden stripes. At one of the nearby bars, some wannabe Jimmy Buffett strummed his guitar and sang about pirates. The music and the moonlight and the wind felt like our best friends.

Trent interrupted the walk with words. Questions. Always questions. What did I want for my birthday? (A visit to FSU's planetarium.) Were we going to see my grandmother? (No.) Did I think Gray would get me a cool gift? (Yes. He'd given me a gift early—a metal stamped necklace with the longitude and latitude of the Fountain of Youth Park.)

"Balls, that's cool," Trent said of the necklace.

We made it to the jetty in about forty-five minutes, sticking close to the shore, even though it was tempting to check out the bird sanctuary when there was no one around to tell us not to. Getting caught by our parents was one thing; getting caught by some surveillance camera was another.

Trent must have known I worried a little about us getting away with this, because he said, "It's your birthday, Sadie May. Even if we get caught, we've practically got a free pass."

He made a good point.

Laughing, we stepped up on the rocks and checked our balance, and it felt like we were walking on water. The ocean lapped around us, and I wondered if the tides were going in or out. After scrambling thirty-five feet down the jetty and being careful with the slick places and the barnacles, Trent sat down and unzipped his backpack.

"We're not going to the end?" I asked.

"No need."

Unsure of what was about to happen, I watched him remove a cigarette, a lighter, and a thermos. I sat down next to him in anticipation.

"Now, what we have here is a unique opportunity." He lit the cigarette and passed it to me.

I didn't have a clue what to do, and I told him as much.

"Just inhale and then blow out."

I did.

I coughed.

He laughed.

I tried again.

I blew zero smoke rings in my two triumphant drags.

He took the cigarette back, puffed one cloud (also not a ring), and then stubbed it out against the rock. "One down," he bragged. "Now, this."

"Are you going to get me drunk, Trent McCall?"

"On a cup of wine? Hardly. This is for the experience. We have the rest of our lives to get wasted."

"Are you going to bring Gina out here for her birthday?"

"Maybe," he said with a wink. "Tonight's your night, little sister."

I loved it when he called me family. Trent and Max weren't just next-door neighbors. Mom and Dad teased that they got stuck with me, but they chose the boys. We'd been fighting and getting in trouble and eating mac and cheese together all our lives. Mac-and-cheese bonds are stronger than blood swears.

Trent twisted the thermos lid and passed me the container. Tipping my nose toward the liquid, I recognized it. Pinot grigio. My parents drank it after dinner, and no self-respecting kid with a box of wine in her fridge resisted sampling the wares.

I took an easy sip and said, "Cheers," even though there were no glasses to clink.

Trent tipped up the thermos and echoed my cheers. He returned it to his pack. "Now, you don't have to do the next part if you don't want, but I totally think we should because we'll laugh our asses off about it someday."

"I'm up for anything."

Trent popped me hard in the biceps. "You sure about that?" He peeled off his shirt.

Skinning. Oh, right. I hadn't asked what he meant by that earlier because I hadn't wanted to know, but now, I had a very good idea.

He slid off his shoes.

He shimmied out of his cutoffs.

"Too far?" he asked.

"Um . . ."

"You don't have to." He shook his head convincingly. "I was only going for the trifecta of adulthood."

"No. I'm game. As long as we get in before we really strip down."

More relieved than surprised, I set to work, removing my shoes, T-shirt, and shorts, until I had a bathing suit that was an underwear edition. We were awkward with a side of awkward. Like two kids at camp who discover the showers don't have doors.

I jumped in first. The water was July-warm and perfect. Trent cannonballed in next to me, laughing as he resurfaced.

"I can't believe we're doing this." I splashed him in the face.

His face pinked. "Gray said the same thing."

Awesome. He'd done this with Gray.

"And you're going to do it with Gina," I said.

He giggled.

I shouldn't have used the words do it.

Trent stopped laughing and said, "Don't tell Gray I told you. Okay? Or Gina."

"Okay."

"Swear," he said, and put out his pinkie.

We swore all the swears we knew.

Trent claimed pinkie swears should be rated R. Then, without further discussion, we turned our backs to each other and took off the rest of our clothes. I held mine in my hand. I'm not sure what he did with his.

There I was, naked with Trent McCall. Technically, I was naked near *Trent McCall, but it seemed like a pretty legit skinny-dip to me.*

"Are we going to turn around?" he asked.

"Don't ask me. This was your idea. You think it counts if we don't?"

"Yep." He sounded truly nervous now.

"What do we do?" I asked.

His voice crawled out of him. "Put our underwear back on?"

We did exactly that, swam back to the rocks and hauled ourselves out, dripping and laughing. "I didn't think you'd strip," Trent said.

"And miss out on the trifecta of adulthood? I don't think so," I teased.

"But we're not going to tell anyone?"

"Naw," I promised.

And I hadn't. Except now, it seemed like I had.

CHAPTER FOUR

I opened my computer, hoping to wind down the night with Max.

The connection at the convent compound where he'd lived for the past eleven months could be pretty sketchy. We were lucky enough to live in the same time zone, but El Salvador didn't do daylight saving time, so he was actually an hour behind me. It was nine forty-five his time. I opened a chat window and waited to see if he would respond. If not, I'd email.

Me: You there?

Three little dots appeared.

Him: Yep.

Me: What's up?

Him: I have a surprise for you.

Me: I need a good one. Rough night around here.

Him: Tell me about it.

I opted to leave him out of the mysterious Big business and go straight to the most worrisome thing on my mind.

Me: My parents are currently the spawn of Satan.

Him: ☺

I laughed. Max and his small victories of making heavy things light.

I explained that they were making me go back to school in the fall and that they wanted me to be social this summer.

Him: What do you think about all that?

Me: It would be easier if you were here.

I didn't want to say too much on the topic because Max felt really isolated.

He'd lost his brother and most of his voice, and then his parents had moved him to a third-world country. On a scale of suck, he topped out pretty high on the charts. Complaining about school—something he dearly missed—would be insensitive.

Him: Well, beautiful, that could be arranged.

I held *beautiful* in the palm of my hand instead of letting it go to my heart. He only said stuff like that because he couldn't see me. Hadn't seen me. I'd told him all about the plastic surgeries and physical therapy, but that didn't translate into an image for him. What would he say when he came home for the anniversary?

Injuries weren't the only obstacles we'd face. Email Sadie was confident. Email Sadie flirted.

Email Sadie wasn't a lie; she was an invention of hope.

So I had to question if the relationship we had here, created in a year's worth of emails, would hold water at home.

I had serious doubts.

That I kept to myself.

Me: Tell me you're coming home tomorrow.

Him: I'm coming home tomorrow.

Me: Don't mess with me.

Him: I'm not. That was my surprise. I'm flying home tomorrow with Mom.

Tomorrow.

Whoa.

Me: :-) Best news ever!

I was incredibly ready to see *him*. I just wasn't ready for him to see *me*.

Him: I know, right? I thought Mom was joking until she showed me the tickets. Can you pick us up?

I couldn't pick him up by myself. Driving a car wasn't something I did. I'd been getting around in my tennis shoes and an old Honda Spree. Even if I did manage to snag a ride, the airport . . . well, I hadn't been in a crowd like that since my last panic attack at the grocery store.

Him: I really meant . . . can you meet us? I know crowds are hard for you. I wouldn't ask if I didn't really want to see you. But if you can't, I'll wait until I get to the house.

The sheer power of his understanding fueled my courage.

Me: One way or another, I'll be there. What time?

We exchanged the details, and I let him go so he could pack.

Max was coming home.

It was the best news I'd had in a year.

Switching off the lamp, I settled under my duvet and stared at the slivers of moonlight slicing through the miniblinds in my room. Light, flying through space, bouncing off the moon from ninety-three million miles away. Crazy-powerful.

Max only had to travel twelve hundred miles tomorrow, but I thought of him the same way: a crazy-powerful light. What would he think of me? I flopped this way and that— worried about his reaction and that whoever had gone through Big might start sharing those notes with other people—before I gave up and retrieved Big from the floor.

"You can stay up here. As long as you keep your beak shut."

Big said nothing, so I nuzzled my face against his, and listened to the ceiling fan turn until late into the night.

CHAPTER FIVE

Some Emails to Max in El Salvador

From: sadiemaykingston@gmail.com

To: tothemax@thecenter.es

Date: July 11

Subject: RE: how are you?

Max,

Thanks for emailing me. I didn't know if you would have internet
or not, but I'm glad you do. I still can't believe you're in El
Salvador. I stare at your house, all vacant and dark, and can't
believe you're gone. Mom said that your mom and dad met in
San Vicente when they were in the peace corps. She wasn't
surprised your dad took the bridge contract when it came up
because it's a good way to go back to who they were before all
this happened.

It might be great for them, but it doesn't feel fair to you. For me, it's too easy to believe Trent's just on vacation.

Typing his name is hard.

Typing anything is hard. My right arm is still in a cast to my shoulder so I'm pecking this out with my left. My words still come slowly at times, but the doctors say my brain is fine. They say I'm lucky. I know you asked how I'm doing, but I'll have to tell you more in the next email. That's not an easy or fast answer.

What about you? How's your voice? Is your vocal cord healing? It must be really hard not to be able to speak. Do people there know about Trent?

Sadie

From: sadiemaykingston@gmail.com
To: tothemax@thecenter.es
Date: July 13
Subject: don't be brave with me, mister

Max,

You said you were lucky that no one there knows. Did you mean that? If no one there knows, then they don't have access to Trent or to who you were with him. That's a shame, ya know?

I keep thinking about all the people I might meet in life, and how they won't know him. And that seems like a whole other tragedy.

Honestly, you sound like you're trying to be brave.

You don't have to do that with me.

In fact, if you need bravery, you've come to the wrong spot.
I'm empty. So what if our emails are the place we set aside to
be honest? And if you're lonely, or scared, or sad, or angry,
or . . . whatever, you say it here, to me. And I'll do the same.

Sadie

From: sadiemaykingston@gmail.com
To: tothemax@thecenter.es
Date: July 17
Subject: RE: don't be brave with me, mister

Max,

You're right. I didn't actually do the same. So here goes:

I'm lonely, and I'm surrounded by people. People who think
they understand, but they aren't inside my head. I feel like I'm
living in the middle of a terrible "You had to be there" story.

Sadie

From: sadiemaykingston@gmail.com
To: tothemax@thecenter.es
Date: July 22
Subject: Where is our prestidigitator?

Max,

True. I'm not living that story alone. We were in the car
together.

   Thank you for telling me how angry you are. Keep telling
me. I might not know what to say, but I'll listen.

   I'd pay a million dollars for a time machine or a magic wand.
I've been a fixer my whole life, and this is unfixable. That's
overwhelming to me.

                                   Sadie

From: sadiemaykingston@gmail.com
To: tothemax@thecenter.es
Date: July 26
Subject: RE: Gina and Gray

Max,

You're right, except you're wrong. Technically, I have Gina and
Gray, but at the same time, I don't. So far, every time we've
been together all we've done is push each other's grief buttons.
Then, it turns into a weird cry-fest, which isn't helpful. So
lately, when either of them visits, I pretend I'm sleeping. That's
terrible, but I'm too tired to cry. Plus, I don't want them to see
me like this. And I really don't want to see them the way I see
them, either.

   Mom says I'm looking better. Of course, Mom is nuts. My
face looks like a cracked desert. The doctors are going to do a

series of plastic surgeries when I'm healthier. I'm hopeful those will help. Maybe then I'll have conversations with my friends, family, and strangers that aren't about my face or the wreck.

It's crazy. In the time we need each other most, we don't seem to know what to do with each other.

The doctors put a steel rod in my arm. If they'd been more considerate, they would have inserted a forget button in my chest. Ah, the limits of modern medicine.

Sadie

From: sadiemaykingston@gmail.com
To: tothemax@thecenter.es
Date: July 28
Subject: Apology Central—How may I direct your call?

Max,

Yeah, I'm not surprised Gina and Gray emailed you. Both of them asked me for your email address. What you said is fine. I would never tell them stuff about you, either. And yes, they say *I'm sorry* like those are the only two words in their vocabularies.

Honestly, I don't want their sorrys. All I want is for them to look at me—to see me the way they used to. I want to believe that who I was for sixteen years is stronger than the picture they have of me now. Can I ever be the crazy, fun girl again?

At the very least, they could stop bullshitting me. I'm tired of them saying, "Sadie, you're looking much better." How would they know? Neither of them will actually look at me, so . . .

Mom says they feel guilty for causing the wreck, which I get, but losing them, and Trent, and even you (in a way) is too much for me right now.

Sadie

From: sadiemaykingston@gmail.com
To: tothemax@thecenter.es
Date: July 30
Subject: RE: No Skype, Please

Max,
The fact that you can't see me helps big-time. It's easier to email someone the truth when you know you don't have to face him. Maybe if Gina and Gray went away, it would help. Maybe I'll go away instead.

You and I didn't hang out as much as Trent and I when you lived next door, but it's nice to have something new that didn't exist before our world hit the spin cycle. Mom says painful events are life's wrecking balls—they make doorways that let some people out and others in. I guess these emails are me putting a welcome mat at the foot of the rubble and whispering, "Max, come on in."

That's scary, but it's helpful. If that is ever too much pressure, let me know. Something about this feels right. Or maybe it just feels easy.

I need some easy.

Other people mean well, but they don't, or can't,
understand. They ask how I'm doing and it's awkward because
I don't have a clue. There are two parts to the question:

1. How am I doing physically?

2. How am I doing without Trent?

I don't know how to answer either. Do you?

As for number two, this is my guess: He was your brother.
He was my friend. I know exactly how you're doing without him.
I take how I feel and multiply times a billion.

                              Sadie

CHAPTER SIX

I humbled myself the next morning and asked for a ride to the airport. That ask went down better than expected. Mom was as ecstatic to see the McCalls as I was. She even offered to straighten my hair and do my makeup—an offer I happily accepted. I'd take all the help I could get.

About forty-five minutes into the process she threw down the eyelash curler and said, "Looking good. You want nail polish, too?"

"Nah, I'll just chew it off."

She smacked my hands away from my mouth. "It's Max. You don't have to be nervous."

"That's exactly why I'm nervous. I don't want to screw this up."

"Flip your head over a few times."

I did as instructed. When I straightened back up, she set a straw fedora on my head and tweaked two rogue strands into place. "Bea*uti*ful," she whispered.

I stuck my feet in a pair of sandals and said, "Let's hope Max agrees."

Mom placed both hands on her hips. "If he doesn't, he's fired."

I laughed and thanked her.

"Hey, it's what I'm here for."

Mom took advantage of getting me out of the house, doting on me, treating me to a meal at the pier (dark, corner booth) and gelato (chocolate). We were almost late to the airport.

Was it against the rules to buy a guy flowers? It was either roses, magazines from the Hudson News stand, or ten bucks toward something sketchy from the refrigerated case. I couldn't show up empty-handed after a year, so I went with the roses. Yellow, because yellow was more masculine than pink.

"Yellow means friendship," Mom said.

"Dammit."

Mom laughed. "Max probably won't know that."

I stared a hole through the arrivals board from my corner of the small waiting area. Mom plopped down in one of those uncomfortable leather seats, tapping her foot while she checked email on her phone. When flight number 4563 from Miami changed from *On Time* to *Landed*, I came and stood next to her. Right on cue, my phone buzzed in my pocket.

Max: **On the ground.**

Me: **Waiting area!**

"You ready?" Mom asked.

"I'm . . . not sure," I admitted. My hands poured sweat, and I wiped them on Mom's shoulders to demonstrate. I figured she used to spit-clean my face in public, and paybacks were a bitch. She gave me an "Oh, gross," but smiled the whole time.

"You look great," she promised.

"We did our best."

To keep from pacing, I tucked into a ball at her feet and smelled the roses. They were sure to make Max laugh—a nice way to kick off his return. Perhaps a distraction from my face.

Max: **At the gate. Warning! I smell like a plane & I sound like an engine.**

Me: **I don't care.**

Max: ***Smiles***

Mom and I stood up, anxious. Sonia appeared first and waved.

"Hey, Sadie! Hey, Tara! I'll be right there." Her voice stretched down the monochrome hallway to greet me before she darted into the women's restroom.

Behind her was Max. I nearly collapsed at the sight of him. When Max left for El Salvador he was five six and 175 pounds; I never dreamed he'd return at over six feet. Stocky and boyish transformed into lean and ropy and . . . sort of hot.

Hot. (adj.) a word I never expected I'd use to describe Max McCall.

The closer he came, the more I realized he looked nearly

identical to Trent. I lowered the fedora, ensuring it fully covered Idaho, and prepared myself for his examination. Max half jogged, half ran toward the security exit and flipped an apologetic wave to the TSA lady guarding the Point of No Return.

I imagined the TSA lady smiling at him, loving her job of witnessing reunited families.

"Sadie." His voice strained to reach above a whisper, but he sounded so happy.

"Max."

There was no hesitation on his part. He threw out his arms as if he were catching the entire sky, and cinched us together.

Instinct took over, and I held him back. The fedora fell off.

Plane smell was a mixture of fajita, sweat, and Max. Plane smelled perfect. I dropped the roses on the fedora and held on all the way to my fingertips. Inside his hug was rough and firm and warm, like a cozy sleeping bag on a January night.

My *You look like Trent* came out as, "You're so . . . tall."

"I'm glad to see you, too." Max lifted me off the ground and swung me side to side. It was such a Trent thing to do, or maybe now it was such a Max thing to do. Regardless, this total smash of muscle-against-muscle friendship was hard to put into words.

I didn't try. I just enjoyed it.

When the hug ended, he latched on to his backpack straps and looked at me. I didn't let him linger. I grabbed my hat and shoved it on my head, checking with Mom for a nod of approval.

She gave it as Max said, "You look amazing."

That gravelly voice worked on me. He meant what he said, but I set my sights on the carpet, unsure of what to say or whether to argue. I had a hat over Idaho, jeans over Pink Floyd, and sleeves over Tennessee. Of the bigger scars, that left the jagged one that arched up from the right corner of my mouth that I'd never named. I'd considered Mississippi, because it was two crooked, jagged lines—a sideways squiggly lightning bolt—but it never stuck. If Max saw all these imperfections, plus other minor ones, then *amazing* wouldn't be his word of choice. Piecing Frankenstein back together took time and money.

Max focused on my eyes. "Seriously, I like the hat."

I switched the subject. "You look . . ." I inventoried Max. Cutoffs; sandals; worn University of El Salvador T-shirt; long, choppy brown hair that the sun had worked on; a dirty FSU baseball cap hanging out of his pocket. It wasn't all those things that struck me most; it was the way they fit him. The way they would have fit Trent: loose in some places, fitted in others.

He flicked his head toward the restrooms. "Mom says it all the time. I didn't want to tell you."

I couldn't argue with that. I hadn't totally warned him about my appearance either.

Mom intervened in our awkwardness. "It's good to have you back, sweetheart."

Max coughed and touched his throat. When he spoke again, his voice was a little louder.

"Hey, Mrs. K. It's good to be back."

Years of neighborly surrogate-mom moments showed in their welcome-home embrace. If Max were Trent, he'd have said something profoundly silly. Max was just Max though, and the hug was enough.

I held my hand up and measured his height. "Good Lord, what have they been feeding you?" I asked.

He laughed. "Beans."

"You're taller than he was," I said.

Max straightened his back and put out his chin, proud of the six or seven inches he'd gained in the past year. "Not by much."

I saw a ghost of Trent put Max in a headlock and tease, "You'll always be my *little* brother." He would've wrestled him down to the floor until Max tapped out.

Shaking away the image, I said, "Well, I guess I can wear any size heel I want around you." Which was total crap; I never wore heels. Still, I popped him on the chest, unable to control my happiness now that the initial meet-and-greet was over. "I can't believe you're home."

"I know, right? My face hurts from smiling," he said, and stretched his jaw.

His voice hurt too. I winced a little for him.

Max's mom manifested out of thin air carrying two shopping bags and a purse made of Kit Kat wrappers. "Tara!" Sonia dropped her bags and gave Mom a hug and then me. Time away had been kind to her. She'd shed four skins of sadness since last June, but she still wore some of it in her eyes and a little more in the gray hair above her ears. Max's messages indicated Operation: Heal the Family had been relatively successful. Still, this trip home must be bittersweet.

"Dad caught a flight on Tuesday," Max explained as I glanced around. He touched his throat, cleared it, and said, "He had some business in New York and had to fly into Panama City."

"Hey, you sound good. Your voice is louder than I expected."

He ignored my compliment the way I'd ignored his earlier. Instead, he picked up the flowers I'd dropped. "You shouldn't have."

"I had to do something."

There are two kinds of laughter: at and with, and Max was brilliant at the with kind.

"You haven't changed a bit, Sadie," he said.

"I've changed several thousand dollars' worth, Max McCall."

Sonia interrupted her son's reply. "I think Max is trying to say the roses are lovely."

I swiped the roses from him and handed them to Sonia, feeling my cheeks turn pink with embarrassment. I wondered what that color looked like against my scar.

"We'll put them in water when we get home. It'll be nice to have that fresh smell in the house." She turned to Mom. "George said the house looked wonderful. Thank you so much for taking care of us."

Mom touched her friend on the arm. "It was a pleasure to help."

The two of them linked arms like sisters and leaned their heads together. Max and I let them walk on ahead of us. He pointed to the Baggage sign and I fell into step with him down the short concourse.

When we arrived at the baggage carousels, Mom split away toward the exit and said, "I'm going to go pull the car up."

Max spotted his mom's bags immediately. He tugged two large crates and three pieces of luggage off the belt and dropped them next to me.

As I stepped away to grab a cart, a little girl, probably three or four, tugged on her mother's shirt. "Mommy, Mommy, what happened to that lady's mouth?"

"Trisha, it's not nice to point," the mom scolded the girl, and shot me a silent *Sorry*.

I shrugged to make the woman feel better, but everyone near us had already caught the spectacle. Great. Love being the local freak show. I made a mental note to stop smiling. Resting bitch-face calmed the scar at my mouth to a thin red line.

Max stroked my back the way Gray once had—in a way I could get used to—and said, "Shake that off. Kids are crazy."

I went with it. "Yep," I said, knowing my bravado failed.

Max pulled me into another full-body tackle-hug.

Somewhere in the distant past, I heard Trent's voice say, "Hold on. Hold on. Hold on."

CHAPTER SEVEN

I ran in my sleep that night—a route much longer than usual. In my dreams, I searched for Ponce de Leon's Fountain of Youth, and I was convinced finding it was the key to everything. I awoke tired until I remembered Max.

He was back, and we were going to hang out. Social time: *A posse ad esse.* He had promised he'd call as soon as he finished everything his mother needed. If I knew Sonia, she'd have him tied up until late afternoon. That meant I had time to go out to the salvage yard.

In the still-dark morning, I scribbled a one-word note— *Out*—for my parents, checked the mailbox—empty—and hopped on my scooter. The scooter was a compromise. Mom and Dad didn't want me dependent on them. I didn't want to drive. Fletcher suggested the scooter as middle ground. So I chose a black Spree and a really expensive helmet. It was—basically—one step above a golf cart, and I drove it like an old man.

It was too damn hot to walk everywhere, so it was a good battle to lose. Plus, the air felt good on my skin. Jenni, owner of the Donut Barista, leaned out the pick-up window of her shack and waved. I cut the Spree's engine, pocketed the key, and left my helmet on to order.

"The Friday usual?" she asked, bubbly as ever.

"Yes, ma'am."

"Coming up in two shakes of a dog's tail. Lovely day, isn't it?"

If today were a category five hurricane, it would still register as a lovely day on her scale. Jenni loved doughnuts and coffee and serving people the way preachers loved long prayers. She wore her heart in her eyes, and I liked her more than I knew how to show. I'd never seen her outside the shack, but I imagined her as a grandmother. At home, she probably wore jeans with an elastic band, a pair of mall-walker white shoes, and answered to little kids who called her Nana.

I liked to imagine things about people.

There weren't many people in my life anymore, so for the few I interacted with, I tried to cultivate real relationships.

"Jenni, you know Max? The guy I've been telling you about."

"Absolutely. He's your sweet honey in El Salvador?"

I nodded. "He came home yesterday."

She howled with delight. "You want to make this a triple?"

"Naw, we're getting together later. I just wanted to tell someone."

She heard how happy I was. Hell, *I* heard how happy I was. It sounded strange.

"You'll have to bring him by." She fitted the lid on one steaming-hot cup of joe and stuck a straw in my iced latte, patting my hand before reaching for my credit card.

I flipped up the visor on my helmet and thanked her. There was something very satisfying about knowing someone in small percentages.

"Thanks, Jenni."

"You are most welcome, Sadie Kingston."

Jenni made note of my whole name on the first day and repeated it once a visit. I added a three-dollar tip to the card. I couldn't afford to do that all the time, but today was special. I felt generous. No envelopes in the mail, Mom and Dad were satisfied with my going-to-the-airport effort, and I was pretty sure I'd get another hug from Max. Maybe more.

Jenni felt generous too. The weight of my doughnut bag equaled more than my order.

Sprinkler systems on the main drag forced me to back streets and the back streets led me into the country. The sun sprinted up the sky, and sweat tickled my back in a matter of minutes. By the time I rolled up to the gates of Metal Pete's Fine Salvage Yard, I'd sucked down half my iced coffee and considered chugging the rest.

"Cool it down, Florida," I pleaded.

Florida stuck out both middle fingers and zapped away the tiny breeze.

I hiked my sleeves to three-quarter length, parked the Spree, and grabbed Metal Pete's breakfast.

The auto salvage business fascinated me. From the road, it looked like an unorganized metal shit-fest. Up close was a different story. Row after row of damaged cars, in various states of decay, took up fifteen acres of land. Every car, truck, RV, school bus, motorcycle, and boat had been inventoried and arranged with customers in mind. I'd been here dozens of times, and the ocean of debris still made me stare in awe and sadness.

"Metal Pete," I called out.

Headlight came instead, tail wagging, and nosed the doughnut bag with interest. "Where's Metal Pete?" I asked her.

Both ears rose into spikes as she trotted ahead to the office. The door was open, and I sauntered in as if I worked there.

"Hey there, you." Metal Pete glanced up at me as he worked some sunblock into his weathered face. "I thought you'd forgotten about your favorite salvage yard."

"Been trying to cut back," I told him. Although he knew I didn't mean it.

I placed his breakfast on a table that had once been in the galley of some yacht, and played with seat-belt riggings that held fern planters. Everything around here got repurposed.

Metal Pete peeked inside the bag, rubbed his nonexistent belly, and said, "Me too."

The man never met a pastry he didn't like, but he walked this place every day, refusing to ride in the Gator the way I'd suggested. The yard was his gym, and it was pretty damn effective. His old never sagged.

"You look different," he said, tossing a doughnut hole into his mouth.

"Max is back."

"And you're here? Kid, I haven't been your age in a long time, but that's not how dating works."

"He's busy this morning, and we're not dating, exactly, we're just . . ."

"Dating," Metal Pete concluded. "And . . . like usual . . . I'm your distraction."

I smiled around my straw.

"Okay"—he drummed his fingers on his cheek—"I'll give you a dollar if you can find a 1998 red Chevy Impala with an intact bumper."

From there, I followed the script of a conversation we'd had many times. "You know exactly where it is."

"Yeah, but you don't, and you, my dear, are looking peaky. Why don't you go wander around in the sunshine?"

"For a dollar?"

"You drive a hard bargain. How about two?"

"Make it five, and you've got a deal," I told him.

This was a game we played. He wanted to pay for his breakfast, and I never let him. Scavenger hunts were a different story. I charged him double for those.

"Give me a hint of which direction to look."

Metal Pete devoured his doughnut in three bites and scratched his chin. "It's close to where you'll end up anyway."

Metal Pete and I understood each other. His wife died of cancer five years ago, and so far, I'd never seen him out of the yard, never seen him in anything but his gray Hanes V-neck, and never seen him interact with anyone who didn't have grease on his hands. Junked metal was easier to sort out than a broken heart. I was his exception and he was mine.

I filled a cup of water and gave the ferns a drink on my way out. "I'm taking Headlight with me."

"Thief," he said.

"Cheapskate."

"Red. Chevy. Impala. Go."

He pointed, and I laughed. We were oddball friends.

I liked to imagine he needed me as much as I need him.

As soon as I rounded the first corner of cars and was out of sight, I stripped down to a tank top and hung my long-sleeve shirt off the busted mirror of an old S-10 pickup. I stood there for a moment, exposed, staring at the sky as if it were a show.

"Good morning, sky," I whispered.

I swear I heard God say, "Bring on the vitamin D."

Okay, it wasn't God, but I liked the idea that the sky was listening. Trent and Gray used to say *Bring on the vitamin D* when

I'd warn them about not wearing enough sunscreen. They'd both worked for Relax Rentals, the company that managed chairs and umbrellas for the high-rise condos on the beach. Gray was probably there today. In a different reality, the one without the wreck, I'd be there helping him drill umbrella holes in the sand or carrying chairs. In this reality, I was in the salvage yard, wishing it was already evening so I could see Max.

But still, I thought about Gray as I walked. How he looked both good and bad the other night at the beach. Fit. Too fit. He needed to lay off the protein and weights until his neck matched his head again.

But what did I know? I wore long sleeves and hung out in a salvage yard. There were certainly worse obsessions than excessive fitness. I guess it all came down to this: even on the days I hated Gray Garrison, I wanted him to be okay.

And he didn't look okay.

I wished I could do something about that, but absolution dangled in front of me like a carrot on a ten-foot pole.

I stopped thinking about Gray and found the Impala. Using some tire grease, I wrote the location on my arm and headed in the direction I'd been going all morning.

Trent's Toyota Yaris.

CHAPTER EIGHT

No matter how often I visited the Yaris, the first glance sent my stomach to my throat.

The metal beast was quiet and picked over, twisted and sad. The front-end damage was so severe there was never much to salvage. Someone had since purchased the backseat, a rear taillight, and the two rear tires. The first time I came to Metal Pete's, he walked me through the yard, offering a warning that it wouldn't be easy to see the car. I wasn't the first survivor to arrive on his doorstep searching for closure.

In an average week, I spent four or five hours lounging in my makeshift tire seat as if it were a raft and this row of cars my lazy river. I was here more than that, playing Karate Kid to Metal Pete's Mr. Miyagi, except without the karate. He ran me here, there, and everywhere, pretending it was the price of sitting time at Metal Pete's Fine Salvage Yard.

I greeted the crushed roof with a sympathetic pat, as if I owed it or someone an apology, and said, "Hello, Yaris."

The Yaris didn't answer.

It had been very vocal on June 29 and silent ever since.

I still told it the truth. "Max is home. I might bring him for a visit."

Seeing the Yaris the first time was as excruciating as Metal Pete had promised, but now, there was no way to look at the twisted heap without thinking, *How did anyone walk away from that?* The Yaris reminded me that Max and I were miracles. Considering that the hood and the front seat were practically one, I hated my scars a tiny bit less.

Coupled with that miracle was guilt, and I searched for an answer to *Why Trent? Why not me?* in every twist of the metal, every tiny rusted flake, every shattered piece of windshield.

When I told Fletcher about my visits to Metal Pete's, he explained survivor's guilt to me and said it was normal. Then he'd asked, "Sadie, do you have a time machine?"

"No."

"So there's nothing you can do to change what happened at Willit Hill?"

"No," I'd said, feeling the trap in his question.

"Then, somehow, you have to accept that you're still here, and that maybe, just maybe, there's a reason. Find the reason."

"Find the reason."

I repeated those phrases, "Find the reason" and "I don't

have a time machine," regularly.

Time machine or no, I had good memories in that car. Gray and I making out in the backseat. Trent, Max, and I going on boiled-peanut runs on Saturday mornings. Gray and I, and Gina and Trent, riding to dinner before the guys' junior prom. Trent made a little magnet for the Yaris that said *Limo*, and we all cracked up because the car was not much bigger than a go-kart. I tried desperately to replace the last memory with those happy ones, so that maybe, I'd get my ass behind a wheel again.

"I will drive again. Right, Headlight?"

Headlight sat down in shade of my shadow and put her nose on the ground. Knocking the dust off her coat, I gave her a good long rub and watched her knobby tail attempt to wag. She reminded me of the cars, the way she limped, looped, and sighed with the effort of walking, and yet she had parts that still worked fine. Metal Pete salvaged more than cars.

"What do you say, buddy? Do you think I can do it?"

Headlight stood up, put two paws on the tire, and licked my cheek.

"Good. I do too," I said, and gave her a scratch between the ears. "But not today. Today, I'm just gonna look."

She settled down and closed her eyes. I followed suit, giving myself permission to remember many other good things about the Yaris.

I didn't hear Metal Pete until he stood over me. He wore a visor bigger than his best grin. Before I could ask, he dropped my long-sleeve shirt into my lap, and I put it on.

"You're roasting like a pig on a spit," he warned.

"I was just thinking."

"Well, think with some SPF." He tossed me lotion from his pocket.

I applied a thick lather of sunblock while he rolled an abandoned wheel rim near me and sat down. I flipped the lotion back his way. "Better?"

"You'll be old someday and I'll be too dead to thank, but you'll remember that Metal Pete's the reason why your skin's still pretty."

Pretty and my skin didn't belong in the same sentence. "I'm *sure*."

"Don't get sassy with me, Sadie Kingston."

"No, sir," I said, knowing Metal Pete's threat was as harmless as Headlight.

"Five dollars for your thoughts?" he said.

"Is that five for the Impala and five for the thoughts?"

His thick shoulders lifted in a half shrug. "It's all Monopoly money anyway."

I tried to keep the fear from my voice. "My folks are making me go back to school in the fall."

Metal Pete toed the bottom of my tire. "Sounds wise of them."

"You're supposed to be on my side."

He held out his hands in an *I call it like I see it* way.

Even though Metal Pete would gladly listen to me ramble

about anything, I read the location of the Impala to him and held out my hand.

A five-dollar bill landed in my palm.

"Thanks," I said.

"Thanks for the doughnuts."

The end of the conversation came the way it often did, with Metal Pete saying, "Well, I guess I'd better get back to the phones. Catch ya next time, Sadie May."

CHAPTER NINE

Some Emails to Max in El Salvador

From: sadiemaykingston@gmail.com

To: tothemax@thecenter.es

Date: August 6

Subject: RE: the video

Max,

I like the video of the convent. Being able to see where you are helps. I imagined something much worse than cinder-block walls, your own room, and McDonald's ten miles away. The shower is pretty old school, but at least you have running water. Can you drink the water there? Have you been sick at all? I forgot to ask in my last email.

You have to climb that volcano mountain. You're not lacking in views. It's beautiful there.

Sadie

From: sadiemaykingston@gmail.com
To: tothemax@thecenter.es
Date: August 8
Subject: Nightmares

Max,

I can't believe they told you just to go on and drink the water and get sick. Ugh. That sounds awful.

I'm glad you brought up the nightmares. No, I doubt they have to do with you being sick. I have them too. I've been having them so frequently that my parents forced me to see a therapist—Dr. Fletcher Glasson—last week. Believe it or not, it wasn't terrible. We mostly did paperwork and, as a first assignment, he suggested I "free-journal" about the wreck.

Do you think it is safe to tell him how I feel? I don't want to write everything down if he's going to tell my parents. These are my feelings and if my parents knew all of them, they'd just worry more than they already do. Fletcher (which is what he asked me to call him) said he wouldn't unless he *had to*. I want to believe him.

Sadie

From: sadiemaykingston@gmail.com

To: tothemax@thecenter.es

Date: August 15

Subject: what I remember about June 29th

Max,

Good idea. But, if I'm going to free-journal with you, then you
have to stop apologizing for letting me take shotgun. You didn't
know we'd crash. Deal? (The problem with writing *Deal* is that
you're in a whole other country.)

Here goes. I remember a lot about that day, but I'll start with
when we got to the cars.

Gina and I hosed off the coolers and stowed them in her
Jeep. You and Trent and Gray strapped the YOLO boards to
the top of the Yaris. Trent mentioned kiteboarding and Gina
said we didn't have to go ninety-to-nothing every day. Trent and
Gina walked back up to the shelter to "discuss" something.

When Trent came back down the walk, he told you and me
to hop in the Yaris, that we were going home. Gina had tears
in her eyes, and Trent didn't crack a single smile. I hugged her
bye and told her to call me after she'd taken Gray home.

Gray leaned into the car for a kiss and whispered, "If they
break up—"

"They won't," I told him.

That was a lie. As much as I wanted us all to be fine, and
be in each other's weddings and other epic crap like that, the

water was draining out of the sink for them. Trent had been . . . restless. He'd told me he'd planned a breakup. Did he ever talk to you about this?

I tried to stay out of it. They were both my friends, and I didn't know what the group would look like if they broke up. I didn't want to take sides, and I was worried they would want me to.

That was the wrong thing to worry about.

The three of us sat in the car for a moment, but I don't remember why. Maybe Trent was on his phone or picking a radio station or just waiting for the car to cool down. My eyes closed in a sleepy way that only a day in the sun can do to you. I tried not to think about whatever Gina and Trent had discussed for twenty minutes at the pavilion. You wanted to roll down the windows, and Trent said it was "too damn hot." Whether it was all the waiting or the sleepiness, I never fastened my seat belt.

Once we were on the road, we sang along to the radio. Not the Eagles, but some old band he loved. They sang "You Shook Me All Night Long," and he went on about how vinyls were back and he wished the Yaris had a turntable. I knew the words to the chorus, but you two knew every verse. I think I gave you shit about it. Do you remember that? Or did I make it up?

After the song ended, Trent brought up St. Augustine and the Fountain of Youth Park. He said he was in an explorer mood.

I said, "Let's go tomorrow," and he said, "Bright and early,

Sadie May. I'll knock on the window."

"Really?"

He nodded, and I remember thinking, *He's serious. We're actually going to road-trip.*

"I'll text Gina and Gray and tell them to take off work."

"Yep," he said, and that made me feel better. Whatever happened between him and Gina at the pavilion wasn't too serious. Yet. The next day we'd all hop in the Yaris and head east to St. Augustine. I closed my eyes and made up a story about us finding the real fountain of youth when we were old and in our thirties. It was probably in some swamp in the Everglades, but we'd have a helluva time looking.

"I think I'm gonna go see if Callahan will let me ride the motorcycle later," he said.

That felt like code-talk to me. "You want me to go with you?" I asked.

"Maybe. I could use some Sadie May perspective."

"As you wish."

I know I said that because Trent loved *The Princess Bride*, and he always gave me a goofy grin when I quoted the movie. Then, I fell asleep. The next thing I remember was our car swerving to the right.

My eyes snapped open. Gina and Gray were stalled out in front of us. My heart rocketed from sixty to a thousand beats, and I grabbed the door handle.

"Hold on," Trent told us.

I screamed.

I never saw the tree.

The Yaris screamed. Metal on bark.

Time either stopped or slowed down, because I remember far too many details from that moment than are possible.

Hold on. Hold on. Hold on. I hear those words in my sleep.

Fletcher asked me to describe that moment. I told him I was a peach in a blender.

Only the pictures afterward and Gina's explanation—the compacted hood, the U-shaped roof—let me understand what happened after the impact ejected me. Gina had stalled the Jeep at the bottom of Willit Hill. Trent swerved to avoid them, and we barreled into a stand of trees.

You were trapped in the backseat. I went flying. Trent . . .

I can't write any more. Sorry.

Sadie

From: sadiemaykingston@gmail.com
To: tothemax@thecenter.es
Date: August 20
Subject: restitution

Oh, Max, I'm so sorry. All this time, I didn't know you were conscious. That you held his hand. You're . . . braver than anyone I know.

Don't beat yourself up. There's nothing you could have done. It's okay to feel. Jesus, I sound like Dr. Fletcher Glasson.

Ignore that shit and do whatever you want.

I just want everything back the way it was. For you. For me. For our families. I want Trent to knock on my window . . . want to get in the car tomorrow and drive to the Fountain of Youth.

Okay, I'm out of juice. I'm going to turn out the light and pretend to sleep.

Sadie

From: sadiemaykingston@gmail.com
To: tothemax@thecenter.es
Date: August 25
Subject: Trent

Max,

I want to go back to your last statement: *I don't think my brother trusted me the way he trusted you. He only told me what he had to.*

Max, Trent absolutely trusted you. As for confiding in you about breaking up with Gina, you can't go by that. There are a million reasons why he hadn't told you he was considering it. Maybe he was embarrassed or something? He always had this idyllic vision of how you saw him, and he wanted to protect that. But more than likely, he wasn't ready to act and didn't want to upset the group chemistry until he understood how he felt.

Sadie

From: sadiemaykingston@gmail.com

To: tothemax@thecenter.es

Date: August 28

Subject: Seafood festival

Max,

Thanks for understanding.

No, Gray and I aren't going to the seafood festival. No need for you to be jealous about missing out on the food. I'm still not going out in public, and Gray . . . well, who knows about him right now.

We wrecked more than the car.

Sadie

CHAPTER TEN

The Social Experiments, as I decided to call them, continued that afternoon. I'd expected a quiet evening with Max—maybe a walk on the beach, some Star Time on the dock, a game of Tell Me Something—instead, I got a joint McCall-Kingston meal. At least Mom and Dad eased me into their high expectations.

Lights shone through every window of the McCall house. Such a strange sight to see after a year of darkness. Sonia had invited us to dinner, her need for community stronger than her weariness from traveling and the need to accomplish a long to-do list. We carried over a key lime pie and a loaf of fresh bread. I carried over some panic, and I wasn't even sure why. I loved these people, and they loved me.

Mom knocked.

"You have a key," I said.

"They live here again," Mom said.

They did. We'd met them at the airport, I'd said hello, and somehow it felt like I was hearing it for the first time.

Sonia ushered us inside, and we re-exchanged hugs. I'd chosen a thin yellow sweater and a pair of ripped-up jeans. My hair was down and half hidden under a straw cowboy hat, but Sonia didn't stand still long enough to look at me. She pushed around boxes with her feet, opened a bottle of wine, apologized for messes that weren't there, and transferred the roses from a table in the foyer to the dining room.

My parents put their hands to work, and I watched. Sonia noticed me loitering and said, "Max is still in his room. Would you go get him?"

"Happy to," I said, and headed down the hallway.

While the McCalls were away, we took care of their house. Dad sprayed for bugs, checked for water damage, and manicured the lawn. Mom cleaned, and changed the vanilla plug-ins every month. Practical stuff. I hadn't helped much. Being in and out of here had made me want to sit at Trent's desk, borrow one of Max's T-shirts, or eat Froot Loops at the kitchen bar. Once I'd curled up in Trent's bed and napped—though I'd never done that when he was alive—and Mom caught me. That little mistake ended my visits. So, when I knocked on Max's door, and he answered with a hoarse "Come in," it felt as if I was seeing a brand-new world.

My eyes roamed over the particulars of his room.

"No more Power Rangers," he said.

"Max, dang. I mean, wow."

"Pretty cool, huh? Dad built it at Christmas."

Plywood board covered in rock-climbing holds consumed an entire wall and part of the ceiling. Mr. McCall's bouldering wonderland hung like a miniature version of the one at my old gym. He'd finally found a use for ten-foot ceilings that didn't involve cobwebs. A small crash mat leaned in the corner, and a pegboard held various clips and things. The rest of the room looked normal: a bed, a dresser, and a closet. Max had Everest and Abercrombie.

"We went to Jacksonville for Christmas," I said. "I didn't even know your dad came home, much less built all this. You never mentioned climbing in your emails or messages."

"I only did it a few times." He stuffed his hands into a chalk bag hanging from a hook. "There were a bunch of crags near the convent and some of the locals took me bouldering. This is . . ."

"Over the top," I finished.

"It's over-something. Dad's . . . had a hard time sitting still. Check it out." Max put his feet on the lowest toeholds, grabbed on, and moved hand-over-hand toward the ceiling. Hanging from one arm, he pulled up and said, "You've got to admit, it's pretty cool."

It was cool.

"You're a monkey," I told him.

He swung down next to me, bumping my shoulder. "I'll

teach you," he offered. "This summer or after school."

I tensed, and he felt it.

Keeping his eyes on mine, he minced no words. "School will be fine. I'll be there."

"You did hear the little kid at the airport, right?"

"Kids are kids."

"Kids are honest." I gave him a good hard poke in the ribs, mustered a happy face, and teased, "Much more honest than you, Max McCall."

"A truth is a truth is a truth, Sadie May."

He ripped those words directly from Trent's repertoire.

"Your mom said supper's ready." I tugged on his T-shirt, flirting a little, and left the room before he argued. He followed me all the way into the dining room, where our parents were laughing about something.

God, that was nice. Max and I paused in the door frame to watch.

"They're . . ." The description escaped me.

"Better," Max finished.

It was the right word. Laughter didn't necessarily mean happy. There were gaps in tonight's meal that laughter could never fill.

Mr. McCall noticed us and greeted me with a warm side-squeeze. He was skinnier and firm in all the places he'd been a little plush. The whole family looked healthier, as if they'd spent their days working out and eating salmon and salad.

"It's good to see you, hon."

"It's good to be here, Mr. McCall."

He tried the old *Call me George* routine, but I was over it. Sonia was one thing; Mr. McCall was another.

"I like the climbing wall you built," I told him.

He gripped Max's shoulder harder than he needed to—Max flinched—and Mr. McCall released him. "Projects are good for the soul," he said, followed quickly by, "Dinner's ready. Wash up."

We'd shared dozens and dozens of meals around this table, but we'd never done it as a group of six. The McCalls had made the decision to move within a month of Trent's death, and there weren't any group dinners, except the one after the funeral. And I was too broken, too out of it, to remember much of that one. Max and I spent the whole time on the deck, away from all the people and their shoulder pats, funeral casseroles, and snotty tissues. I watched the neighbors hug my parents, not knowing what to say. I wondered if they thought it might be better to lose a child than to be left with one as monstrous as me.

I counted the chairs as we moved to our places. Someone, probably Sonia, had had the good sense to remove Trent's chair, the one that used to sit between Max and me.

We made this first transition without tears, but that changed when Mr. McCall asked Max to pray. He chose the grace I'd heard Trent give a million times. His raspy voice sounded nothing like Trent, but it was a beautiful prayer.

"God, we thank you for this food, for rest and home"— Max paused, his fingers flexed against mine—"and all things good. For wind and rain and the sun above. But most of all, for those we love.''

You're supposed to close your eyes when you pray, but I didn't. I held Max's hand the way I used to hold Trent's, and watched for falling tears. There were several. Some of them were mine.

I double-squeezed his hand, an unspoken *You did good*.

He double-squeezed back and whispered, "Been trying to get through that prayer all year.''

Stories were passed around the table like bread and pie. Thankfully, no one talked about rehab or scars or paralyzed vocal cords. Mr. McCall told us about the bridge construction crews he'd worked with every day. By the sound of it, that contract had been a godsend. Sonia, a nurse, had found a place in the community as a midwife.

"Bringing babies into the world is always breathtaking, even in dirt-floor shacks. Being needed that much is a glorious thing,'' she declared.

She was a beautiful delight in that moment, resilient and strong. I envied her.

Max shared things he hadn't mentioned in his emails or IMs. Soccer, a little boy named Dixon, and helping build houses for people in an HIV community near San Vicente. Guilt doubled back and crawled up my spine and into my throat. The McCalls had spent the year finding their reasons to move forward, and I'd barely found my way out of my room. Trent had been their son and brother. What was wrong with me? I had no business being this stuck.

"Where are you going next, George?" Dad asked. "Any other contracts?"

"Next one is local, a small bridge near Miramar. I scoped the area yesterday morning on my way in from Panama City. I might take one in the northeast next year after Max goes to college."

Dad tossed his napkin on his plate. "George, I can't believe you were back on Wednesday and didn't tell us. Can't believe I didn't see one of your lights on."

Mr. McCall wore a proud smile as he said, "I slipped in quiet as a mouse. Knew Max wanted to surprise Sadie."

George McCall winked at his son.

Max winked back and rocked his chair sideways toward me. "It was a good surprise. Right, Sadie?"

I nodded as Sonia said, "Four on the floor."

Max rested the chair legs on the hardwood and teased Sonia. "Mom, we aren't little kids anymore."

The teasing fell short when he looked at the space between us—where Trent used to sit—rather than at me, and I knew he was thinking he shouldn't have said *we*. Everyone at the table knew.

And thought about Trent.

Who always rocked his chair on two legs.

Sonia rescued us, turning the conversation away from Trent to town news and old friends.

I tuned them out after that and didn't tune back in until

I heard my mother agreeing with Sonia that we—me, Max, Mom, and Sonia—would all go shopping the next day.

Not wanting to be impolite, I made direct eye contact that screamed *NO* at my mother and waited for her to retract the invitation. She didn't. The Social Experiment struck again.

"Mom, I thought you said we had something else to do tomorrow."

She knew exactly what I was driving at, and ignored me completely. "Oh, everything else can wait. You and Max both need stuff. It'll be fun to go together." She overemphasized the word *fun*, so I overemphasized my scowl.

"May I be excused, please?" I asked.

Mom and Sonia looked at each other—secret mom Morse code—but she said, "Of course."

I told everyone good night, thanked the McCalls several times for a lovely dinner, and pushed in my chair.

"You're leaving before pie?" Sonia asked.

"I need to go for a run."

Max gave me the *You okay?* question in a blink. He hadn't said much in the past ten minutes, and I assumed his voice needed the rest.

"See you tomorrow." I touched his shoulder as I walked by.

When I got to the beach fifteen minutes later, Gray was there.

I smiled when I saw him, and then I stopped myself.

"I don't have a time machine," I whispered before I walked over to the dune.

He hugged me, quick and uncomfortable—a cordial hand-shake between countries at war. "Hey, I hoped you'd be out here," he said. "I didn't know what time you usually came so I just stayed here after work."

He'd been there since four thirty.

"I'm never here before dark," I said, immediately regret-ting that I told him. What if he made a habit of showing up like this?

"I wanted to see you," he said. "The other night, plus the anniversary . . . it's just, I don't know . . . on my mind. You're always on—" The wind grabbed the rest of his sentence.

"You okay?" I asked.

"Sure . . . I'm always okay, I guess."

Sad eyes and still stoic. Which annoyed me. Why couldn't he just say how he felt rather than cloaking it in some terrible bravado?

"What about you?" he asked.

I gave him honesty. "I lost okay a long time ago."

"I didn't help with that."

"Not so much," I said.

We walked closer to the ocean and sat in that magical place that was dry on our butts and wet on our toes. Gray loved that place best, and it was my habit to do what he liked without thinking about it. Without asking, he untied my ten-nis shoes, slid them and my socks off, and set them behind us.

I didn't comment, but I didn't stop him. I tugged the edge of my shorts lower and waited on whatever it was he had to say.

He derailed a crab from crawling our way and then asked, "You talked to Gina?"

"Not since the other night." I let my eyes slice him a few times before I asked, "Have you *talked* to Gina?"

"We're still friends, Sadie. You should try it."

"I did. Didn't work out so well." Which wasn't completely true, but it felt good to say.

"Jeez, lay off us, will you? I've told you a million times it wasn't like that."

It was like something.

"Gray, why are you here?"

He slid his hand closer to mine in the sand until we were nearly touching. "Gina said you and Max were . . . I dunno . . . together. I wanted to check in, I guess."

"Max and I are . . ." I didn't know the term for what we were. "Close."

Gray exhaled. "I wish I could go back and do so many things over."

His voice dripped with earnestness. All of my firsts were with Gray Garrison, and I remembered them now as if they were a Pinterest board of images. The first time I thought he was cute. The first time I realized he liked me. The first time I realized I liked him back. The first time he'd held my hand. The first time we'd found the perfect make-out place. The first time.

From a distance, he resembled most guys. The kind you might walk by on the sidewalk, but if he was playing volleyball, sandy and shirtless, you'd turn around and watch. Up close, Gray was somewhere between pretty and handsome. A solid cute. He didn't have cool hair or expensive clothes, but he had a sexy voice, long eyelashes, and a curious smile. Thank God for those uneven ears. Those slight imperfections kept him humble. Kept him from thinking every girl wanted him, even though plenty did.

If I leaned in, would he kiss me? I didn't want him to; I wanted *him* to want to.

He turned toward me. His lips were so close.

"You still think about us?" he asked, eyes on the sand.

"Not anymore."

Such a lie. I'd written *Forgive Gina and Gray* in the sand for months.

"I effed up everything, and I can't even really explain it."

"Give it a try."

"It's complicated," he said.

"What isn't?"

"Can I just ask you a question?"

"Sounds like you just did."

He threw a handful of sand at my leg. "You've been mad at me and Gina for . . ." His voice fell away. "But have you ever considered that I might have felt the same way? Before. That sometimes you and Trent looked—"

"Gray, I've told you before that there was nothing between me and Trent."

"But there was," he argued.

"He was practically my brother."

Gray grabbed my hand. "He told me stuff, Sadie. He said he was going to break up with Gina. Hell, he half told me it was for you. Like it was a warning. The day of the . . . accident, when I brought it up, you said they wouldn't, but that was a lie, and we both know it."

Trent, dammit, why aren't you here? Why did you leave me to deal with this? "You've got it all wrong," I said.

"That's what *he* said."

"Well *you* misunderstood."

"Maybe you're lying now."

In a way I was.

"And now you're with Max?" he asked. "That's as effed up as me and Gina. What gives?"

"My life is none of your business anymore." I grabbed my tennis shoes and stood up.

"You know, I used to be jealous of everyone," he admitted. "Trent, because he lived next door. Gina, because she got to have sleepovers with you and listen to all your secrets. Hell, I was even jealous of your parents. They got to be in the house with you every night. I loved being with you. Even after. When you'd pretend to sleep instead of talking to me. I just wanted you to know I was there. But you turned to Max."

"You turned to Gina," I snapped.

We spoke at the same time and said the same thing.

"He understood."

"She understood."

Gray couldn't leave it at that. "That night on the beach," he said. "The night you caught us kissing."

"You were on top of her."

Gray dug his hands into his dark hair. "Yeah, I know. Not that it matters now, but we didn't sleep together. It was only that one kiss, and I was wasted. And you should know"—Gray chewed on one of his knuckles—"she punched me afterward. We were just talking about Trent and she said she was lonely and I said I was lonely and then all of a sudden I was kissing her. And then, I'll be damned if you weren't there watching."

If words could give someone vertigo, these made my world swim. "Are you drunk now?" I asked.

"Maybe a little," he admitted. "All I'm saying is, don't be mad at Gina. I was the *cheating asshole.*" He pulled that quote from one of my past verbal assaults.

"I was lonely too," I said. I wanted to grab him by the shirt and yell, *Look at me!* but I didn't. So I turned off my anger and asked, "Gray, why are you telling me this now? We've both moved on. There's no magic time machine."

"No, there's not." He sounded very sober. "I've been worried about you, Sade. And maybe Max will make you happier now that he's back, but I can't get you off my mind."

"I don't need checking on."

"Maybe you don't . . . but maybe I still need to check. You were my life for . . . most of my life."

Then he said the magic, terrible words.

"I still love you, Sadie Kingston."

What was I supposed to do with that? I mean, I still loved him, too, in a way—how could I not? But, this was the one area in which I'd made forward progress. I wanted to protect that.

The three words I said were not the *I love you too* he wanted. "I gotta go."

He caught my arm, just above Tennessee, the scar at my elbow. Before I could stop him, he closed his eyes and kissed me hard on the mouth.

"I've wanted to do that for months—"

"But you didn't until now." Pain replaced my anger. "Do you know how that felt?"

Do you know how it feels that you, you of all people, won't look at me?

"I couldn't deal," he admitted. "But Sadie, if you need me . . ."

How nice to have the option of not dealing! I held his eyes for two seconds with a stone-cold gaze. "I needed you eight months ago. I'm a little over it now."

If we kept having conversations like this, I'd be writing *Forgive Gina and Gray* for the next decade.

CHAPTER ELEVEN

I woke up the next morning before everyone in my house, but not before the sun. The run from last night must have done its job better than I expected. After I left Gray, I ran farther than I'd ever gone, before turning around.

Gray's words swam through my brain. *I still love you, Sadie Kingston.*

When he said that, I remembered the boy I'd fallen in love with rather than the one who hurt me.

It took me a long time to tell Gray I loved him—five years, to be exact—but I knew it the summer after fourth grade. It happened at a paint-your-own-pottery camp. I roamed through various summer camps in elementary school—everything from surfing to creative writing to science. Mom needed somewhere to put me while she worked, and I needed something to obsess over.

I've always been a tad obsessive.

Gina and I read about the class in the school newspaper and convinced our parents to sign us up. That was a tipping point for Trent. He'd had his eye on Gina since she'd beaten him in a race on Field Day. Trent convinced Gray that pottery class wouldn't be too lousy, and our four mothers happily sealed the deal during one of their Wine-Down Wednesday book clubs.

One thing followed another followed another, like ants on their way to a picnic.

Gray was really skinny. He had an older sister, Maggie, and he wore her Marvel T-shirts. Being an only child, and having no T-shirts to thieve, that was super cool to me.

I set down my book and told him I loved comics.

He told me his mom read him the book I was reading. I'd read Where the Sidewalk Ends *dozens of times, but I kept that to myself.*

When Gray chose the seat next to me, I was glad he was there, rather than sad that Gina was at another table. That week I painted five things—one for each day. Gray painted one. It was a vase with a Where the Sidewalk Ends *poem and drawing on it.*

Secretly, I coveted that vase. I wished I'd thought of the idea, but I wasn't a copier.

The last day, when we were allowed to take our pottery home, Gray didn't show up to class.

All those hours he'd spent perfecting lines and painting and repainting the picture of the sidewalk broke my heart.

"What will happen to Gray's?" I asked the teacher.

"We'll put it on the sale wall. It's really good. Someone will buy it."

I stuck out my lip and promised my mother an extra week of sweeping sand out of the foyer. She bought Gray's vase for five dollars.

The night of our first date, four years later, I tried to give it back to him.

He laughed and said, "Pass me your cell phone."

He directed the light into the vase's small opening.

I read the scratches.

For Sadie.

"I didn't know how to give it to you, so I told my mom I was sick," he said, his face growing as red as a hazard flag.

"You could have just kept it for yourself," I told him.

"No, I couldn't. It was always yours."

After our relationship ended, I'd thrown out the love letters and theater ticket stubs and given him back his T-shirts in a box. I'd kept the vase.

I still love you, Sadie Kingston.

I huffed.

On the bedside table were all the things Max had mailed me over the past year. I liked everything I saw—maybe I'd ride over to Willit Hill and throw the vase into the woods. After all, that was where the sidewalk ended for us.

It was far too early to think that much.

I poured a glass of orange juice and jogged out to the mail-box, enjoying the solitude of six a.m. on our street. Between the house and the end of the driveway, I convinced myself the mailbox would be empty.

I changed my mind when I tugged open the door. Another envelope with my name typed across the front was inside. I treated it like poison. Lifting it by the corner, I walked quickly back to my room so I could look at it and Big at the same time.

The typing and placement were the same as before. The secret was new.

```
I dared Gray to jump off the Destin Bridge. It
backfired. He double-dared me to jump with him.
So we did.
—From a friend
```

I didn't think anyone else had known about that. People, mostly Air Force guys, jumped off the bridge pretty regularly. It was dangerous, and illegal, but the cops rarely found out in time to stop it. As a confession, this was fairly innocuous. But still, someone had been through my stuff, and that made me want to throw knives.

"It doesn't make any sense," I said aloud.

From a friend? Bullshit. A friend would talk to me. A friend wouldn't jerk me around like this. A friend wouldn't invade my privacy.

Someone close to me had rummaged through Big, and I couldn't wrap my mind around why, much less who. If his or her motive was good, in some distorted way, why was he or she picking these particular memories from Big's arsenal of thoughts? He or she had to be picking specific things. I was convinced of that. But skinny-dipping and bridge-jumping? Those were hardly blackmail-worthy events. Was the culprit leading up to something else?

Both of those nights were fun.

Was that the point of this?

Regardless, I added this note to the first one and put them between the pages of an old book. Even with them out of sight, I couldn't sweep the questions from the corners of my mind.

Gray *randomly* appearing on the beach last night, telling me he still loved me. Was that a coincidence? He knew exactly where our spare key was. Knew I jotted down ideas and memories and put them inside Big.

It could be him.

Except this didn't feel like him.

Gray was many things; theatrical wasn't one of them. Trent could have hatched something like this, but Gray was a straight shooter. This was sideways and cockeyed.

I worried it was Max. Thanks to our emails, he had more than enough information to pull this off.

Stop following. Start leading. Here was an opportunity. I needed to eliminate someone as a suspect, and I'd start with

Gray, the *friend* I could afford to lose. Throwing on a pair of crops, a loose long-sleeve shirt, and a straw hat, I hurried back outside.

Three claps greeted me from the McCalls's back porch hammock. Max lowered his graphic novel and waved.

Gosh, he looked like Trent. Except Trent hadn't been a reader or a sci-fi fan. Trent would be paddleboarding or fishing at the pier or renting a kiteboard or something else outside to offset the impending threat of attending college away from the beach.

"You're up early," I said, heading over to Max's porch so he wouldn't have to strain to speak.

"Jet lag. What about you?"

"Life lag," I said with a laugh.

"You're not bailing on shopping, are you?"

"I wish. I'm running out to see . . ." I didn't lie to him. "I need to ask Gray something."

Max pressed the novel flat against his chest and raised his eyebrows. "You sure about that?"

"I'll make short work of it."

He kept most of his thoughts to himself and instead chose to quote one of my emails to him from last October. "Remember, the edge of darkness is one sand-filled step after another looking for the right thing in the wrong place."

"I know. I know."

When I'd cried my heart out last October, all the tears ended up on Max's virtual shirt. After living through the Gina and Gray betrayal, I didn't want Max to think this trip to visit Gray was romantic in nature. I also didn't want to pony up about the letters. Not yet. Not while I still suspected everyone.

"This is a business call," I said.

"You promise?"

I put my hand on Max's shoulder and walked my fingertips up to his chin, skimming lightly over his neck. My touch brought sunshine to his dark eyes. The intimacy of that action didn't strike me until I imagined him doing the same to me.

His hand near my mouth. His fingertips touching Idaho. His mouth on mine. I liked to imagine things like that. Imagination was a gift I kept in my front pocket.

"Hmm," Max said as he laid his hand over mine. We sighed ourselves into a pair of smiles. "Do I get the rest of that later?"

So far we'd made the jump from emails to flesh better than I'd expected. Now, if I could just keep my shit together and be normal . . . "We'll see," I said playfully.

"Hurry back."

"I'll try."

"My mother hasn't been to a mall in a year. I'll never get her out of there without reinforcements," Max said.

Mom and I had argued about the mall last night. Much like the home-schooling discussions, I lost with flying colors.

"Don't worry. My attendance is mandatory," I told him. "Spawn of Satan, remember?"

He changed his tune when he saw how anxious I was. "It won't be that bad."

"Says you."

"I'll get you out of there if you need me to."

"How?"

"Who knows? Shoplifting. Choking. I'll tell Mom I have to drop a deuce."

We both laughed.

"I hope it doesn't come to that," I said.

He raised his novel and said, "Me either. Now go, so you can come back."

CHAPTER TWELVE

The trip to the beach took all of five minutes and an eternity. People were out enjoying their weekend. Joggers and walkers and bikers with bells. Military hard-asses and women in spandex. Old people in golf carts.

I tucked my chin and sped up, remembering Fletcher's insight into my paranoia about being in public.

"Sadie, the whole world doesn't get up in the morning just to watch you," he'd said. "They have songs on their iPods, worries at work, relationships that suck, kids to feed. Most of them don't have time to consider your scars."

I'd argued that might be true for people *his age*—I'd stuck that knife in deep—but my friends were visual. We were a tattooed generation of Instagrammers. Hell, we invented the selfie.

His answer: I wish you would take a selfie.

My return: Maybe I will.

I would not be taking a selfie today.

In an hour, the beach would be full of more eyeballs. Thankfully, Gray was alone, setting up chairs and umbrellas.

I toed off my flip-flops and left them on the wooden walkway, watching Gray carry a load of twelve chairs in a box formation. This job suited him—it required someone strong enough to lift and charming enough to get the tips. The stretch between the Worthy Wayfarer and Blue Waters had been Gray's territory since he was old enough to work.

Sweat dripped down his back as he set the chairs in place and came back for another load. He was fast and efficient, unaware of anything but his job. I waited to walk down until he started setting umbrellas. He drilled a hole in the sand with a bit longer than my leg, dropped in the umbrella, and popped it open against the wind. Gray was about to add the rubber band that kept it closed to the others around his wrist when I automatically stuck out my arm.

He slid the rubber band over my hand.

"I certainly didn't think I'd see *you* today," he said.

I shrugged and played it cool.

He set down the drill and tugged on my shirt. "Wish you'd go back to short sleeves," he said.

I stared at the sun until I saw spots. "I'm used to it."

"You want to make yourself useful?"

I didn't, and I did. I'd promised Max this would be a quick visit, but probing Gray for information too quickly would be a mistake. Staying would make him more amiable.

I nodded.

We tag-teamed the beach the way we'd done in the past, him carrying chairs to locations, me setting them up. Him opening umbrellas, me wearing the rubber bands. We finished before the first families brought down their coolers and wagons of beach crap. Gray dusted off two chairs for us, put his clipboard on his lap, and grabbed water bottles and lotion from his backpack. "You need sunscreen?" he asked.

I did. The rays were terrible, and I'd already been out too long without SPF. Add that to yesterday's burn, and I was on my way to lobsterdom. "Bring on the vitamin D."

"That's right," he said happily.

I accepted the lotion and noticed how he still wouldn't meet my eyes. That didn't keep him from flirting, though.

His smirk lit his face. "You need some help with that lotion?"

I wasn't about to let him rub down Idaho or Tennessee or any of my other scars. Shoving him away with a laugh, I said, "I got it."

"See, don't you like the way that works?" He slid his chair closer to mine.

"What?"

"Me flirting. You laughing." His hand landed on my elbow

again. The same way it had been last night when he kissed me. I jerked away, not so hard that it looked rude, but hard enough to send a signal.

"Gray, you know I'm with Max."

He passed back the water, released my elbow, and asked, "Why'd you come down here then?"

Now or never.

"So," I began. "Any chance you put something in my mailbox recently?"

"Huh?" He lowered his cheap aviator sunglasses and stared directly at the left side of my face. "Like what?"

"Don't play with me. You either did or you didn't."

"Jeez, Sade, you don't have to be all locked-and-loaded every time we're together."

"I'm not all locked-and-loaded. It was a simple enough question."

"Then, I'm not telling you if I did until you tell me what was in your mailbox."

"An envelope."

"Wow. Now, there's a stretch."

"Don't be a jerk," I said, even though he wasn't being a real jerk, and I *was* a little locked-and-loaded.

"Just tell me," he said, drawing on all his patience.

"I can't."

"Can't or won't?" That question had an edge to it.

I ignored it and asked my own. "Did you ever tell anyone we jumped off the Destin Bridge?"

"No." He lifted his hand into the air. "Scout's honor."

"You weren't a Boy Scout," I reminded him.

"Not a liar, either."

He said that, but then stared at his toes, flexing them up and down in the sand until he'd buried them in the white crystal beach. "You remember that night?" he asked without looking up.

"The night we jumped off the bridge?" I asked, a half smile already forming on my face. I wiped it away.

"Yeah."

"Of course I do."

Every. Single. Thing.

"I liked that night a lot," he whispered.

I don't know why, but I wouldn't give him the satisfaction of agreeing. And then I made it worse.

"You jump off the bridge with anyone else?" I asked.

"Why do you do that?"

"Do what?" I frowned at him.

"You stab the happy the second it's in sight."

"I'm pretty sure, of the two of us, I am not the one who stabbed the happy."

His facial features fell like dominos: eyebrows down, eyes closed, dimples flattened, chin lowered into that thick neck. He lifted his collar to his hairline, giving himself a short break from the sun. Or a short break from me.

I leaned back in my chair and stared off toward the pier. Maybe he did the same. Maybe he teared up. Maybe he thought about his plans for the evening.

"Well, I've got to go—"

"Check on the renters," I finished, without turning toward him.

He tapped his clipboard and stood up. When he was four feet away, he turned around and came back.

"Two things."

I knew before he put up two fingers that my straight shooter was back in town.

"One, I don't care about your damn mailbox. And two, I didn't."

"Didn't what? Put something in the mailbox?"

He shook his head at me, as if he couldn't believe I didn't understand the reference.

"I haven't jumped off the bridge with anyone but you."

He walked away.

"Gray."

He kept walking.

I raised my voice. "Gray."

Either the wind ate my words, or he didn't care. I wouldn't chase him. Not into the horde of people. And I didn't want to. Chasing someone was a lovers' game.

CHAPTER THIRTEEN

Two hours later, I'd thrown away all the rubber bands, had a pile of discarded clothes on my bed, and hadn't settled on a hairstyle that covered Idaho or Nameless. I even made Sonia, Max, and Mom sit in the van for ten minutes before I coaxed myself to join them.

"Sorry for the delay," I said, taking the empty shotgun seat.

"It's no problem," Sonia said dismissively. She was busy riding Max's ass about his shopping list.

"Mom, I didn't make a list."

"How do you know what you need if you don't have a list?"

"I have a you," he said, rolling his eyes at me in the rear-view mirror.

Mom didn't ask me about my list. Smart lady.

According to Sonia, Max's clothes were ratty. I thought

they had character; she thought they were overdue for a trip to Goodwill.

My mind didn't make a list or worry about Max's. It was busy as a waterwheel, turning over and over the question of whether Gray had or hadn't put the envelopes in the mailbox. Nearly everything he'd said had been cryptic and inconclusive. But that was a product of us these days, and not necessarily related to the anonymous mailings.

When traffic on the Destin Bridge came to a standstill, I stared out the window, daydreaming. Crab Island, a shallow place in the bay where boaters liked to float and party, lay to my left. To my right, the east and west jetties stretched toward each other like two index fingers. I loved the bridge, and this view reminded me of bridge-jumping. And skinny-dipping.

And who in holy hell was sending those envelopes?

If it wasn't Gray, it had to be Gina or Max.

Both were strong possibilities.

Gina had been trying hard to reconcile for months.

Max was a quiet fixer.

Either of them, if they'd found some way to access Big's belly, were inventive enough to have done this. Max was in El Salvador when I got the first letter, so that put Gina higher on my list, but . . . I'd written all of the thoughts before he left, and his dad was home the day I got the first letter. One walk to the mailbox across the street and George McCall could have put an envelope in there for Max. Easy-peasy. He'd even said at dinner that Max had wanted to surprise me. They'd winked at their secrets.

Whether it was Gina, Gray, or Max, there was no point in spending the day frustrated. Shopping was bad enough. The needle in my brain scratched obediently to the next track, and my eyes drifted toward the spot on the bridge where Gray and I had held hands, said a prayer we wouldn't die, and jumped.

Forty feet.

We kept our hands together until just before we hit the water, and then we slapped them to our sides, staying as pencil-straight as we could.

He yelled like a happy hooligan. I watched the surface rush up on us. We fell forever.

We remembered to do what the soldier told us. "Blow bubbles," he'd said. "'Cause once you hit the water, up isn't up anymore. Down is up, sideways is up, anything is up. The water will lie to you. Let out a few bubbles and follow the bubbles; you'll reach the top."

I frogged to the surface ahead of Gray, drawing air as if I'd never tasted it before. He broke through beside me, slung back his hair, and said, "Damn, that took my breath away."

Gray did other things that night that took my breath away.

"Sadie?"

Mom's voice lured me away from the memory.

"Yeah," I said.

"Don't 'yeah.' Just tell me. Would you like to do that?"

"Ma'am?" I realized she'd been talking to me for a while, and I hadn't heard any of it.

Her thumbs danced on the steering wheel; she pinched her lips a few times before she spoke. "Would you like to have Maria cut you some bangs?"

"What?"

"I don't know why I didn't suggest it sooner. It might make you feel less"—she lowered her voice as if I might not want her to speak the words in front of Max and Sonia—"self-conscious."

I widened my eyes and attempted a joke. "Are bangs the new black or something?"

"Max." Mom sounded downright exasperated. "Please tell her it will be fine."

"Mom, don't drag him into this. If it were fine, you wouldn't be suggesting bangs."

"Oh, shush."

We whipped into Maria's studio, and I got bangs. Just like that. Sonia made Max get a cut, maintaining that he also needed a new style. She was pretty emphatic that he wouldn't be doing his own hair with kiddie scissors anymore.

Our moms and their damn style.

Post-cuts, Max and I took a walk of solidarity down the bathroom hallway. Partly to brush the hair from our clothes. Partly to bitch.

"Dammit, don't I look like prepubescent Joker?" I mocked,

widening my smile with my index fingers as I exited the bathroom.

"You look classy—Audrey Hepburn–ish," Max said. "I'm
the one who got weed-whacked."

"Audrey is a goddess. And had dark hair." Rather than con-
tinue that complaint, I reached up and stroked his hair—what
was left of it—forward. "Sorry. I'm sure it was a sympathy cut."

"Nope. That woman has plans to renovate me. Just you
wait. She's about to put me in Vineyard Vines and Sperrys
when all I want are T-shirts and cutoffs. I already have those."

"You sound like Trent."

"Trent loved surfer clothes." He palmed his head and
laughed. "I should've had Maria bleach my hair blond."

"He had the best hair," I said.

"God, he should have. He spent hours on it." Max sidled up
to the closest mirror and pretended to primp.

We both grinned, but didn't go so far as to laugh. We'd
talked about Trent and we were upright. Not bad. Not bad at
all.

Our mothers wanted us upright and in the van. There
were sales to find and clothes to buy. We hurried along only to
wait in Saturday traffic. This presented me with plenty of time
to examine my new bangs without Sonia or Mom watching.
Yes, I looked younger, and that sucked. I wasn't Audrey, but
Idaho—what Idaho? Bangs were a good idea.

Just so she'd know, at the next red light I got Mom's

attention. Pointing to my forehead, I mouthed the words *Thank you.*

Mom's face exploded with happiness. I loved her pretty well all the time, but I rarely thanked her. I liked to imagine she knew I was grateful, but I wasn't sure parents saw thoughts as well as they pretended they could. If they got occasional glimpses, they probably only saw the worrisome stuff. Maybe if I doubled down every now and again, it would make up for the dry stretches.

"Whew, tourist season," Sonia said from the back.

You're welcome, Mom mouthed back. Then without missing a beat, she answered Sonia. "This traffic is awful. Sometimes it's better to stay home."

"I recall mentioning that," I said.

She sparred back. "Come fall, do you want to go to school in your pajamas?"

"Mom, fall's a long way from now. We didn't have to ruin today."

"We'll be in and out like a flash," she promised.

In and out meant hours of trying on clothes in which someone examined me and said, "Those look great," or "Don't buy that," and doubled my self-consciousness.

Sonia leaned toward the front. "Sadie, are you doing any camps or sports or plays this summer?"

"No, ma'am."

"Max said you've become quite the runner. I thought you might sign up for the Sandblaster 5K."

"Oh, that's a good idea." Mom tag-teamed with Sonia. Her enthusiasm made it sound as if they'd planned this, and I thought twice about those extra thank-yous. They'd baited me, and it rang of Social Experiment training.

"I'll think about it." Better to agree now than let them badger me all day.

"Max is planning on doing Pirates and Paintball," Sonia continued.

I turned around in my seat, surprised. "You are? You didn't say."

"We always have. I was going to ask you," he said.

"I think we should all keep the tradition," Sonia announced. "A true McCall, Kingston, Garrison, Adler weekend. The boat. Camping. You kids playing paintball in the competition—"

"Y'all having adult beverages," Max said as he mimed turning up a bottle for his mother.

Sonia popped him on the leg. "Oh, please. You act like we're a bunch of sots," she complained lightheartedly, and then continued talking about all the fun we'd have together. I faced the front and sank deeper into my seat. Anything that put Max, Gina, Gray, and me together without Trent sounded more like torture than camping. Max sent an apology through the rearview mirror.

The outlet-mall scurry was unbelievable. My anxiety compounded as we searched for a parking place and maxed out as Mom beeped the door locks. The airport trip had been a hill of social anxiety; this was a mountain. Tourists were everywhere.

Mom put her arm around my shoulder. "You're pale, kiddo."

"I know." Pale isn't always a color; it's that hollow-cheeked feeling.

"You need a Gatorade before we start this?" she asked.

Sugar and electrolytes sounded like a plan.

"If you're going to wear sleeves, you have to stay hydrated," she said in my ear.

I nodded and took cash for the vending machine. If Sonia and Max thought my behavior was off, neither of them judged me. Max joined me for a drink, and when we tossed our bottles, he held out his hand.

Sometimes a hand is an anchor. His held me to the world.

In his raspy voice, he asked, "You okay?"

I shouldered off a tear. "Who in their right mind is scared of an outlet mall?"

He pointed at a half-dozen minivans in the parking lot with men sitting in the front seats. "All those dudes."

His joke broke through my stiffness.

We were holding hands. His hands were different from Gray's. Less callused, longer.

I was different when I was attached to him.

I was better.

Don't screw this up, I told myself.

Mom and Sonia walked out of a shoe store and joined us. I wasn't sure what our moms thought about us holding hands, but they didn't embarrass us. Sonia said, "I thought we'd start in PacSun," and Max said, "Let's go."

Four stores and three shopping bags later, I'd successfully maneuvered around trying anything on. I picked something out; Mom swiped her card. The American teenage dream at work. We were on jeans now, and they required a fitting room. I hadn't bought pants over the past year, even though everything I had was too big on me. Weight loss had been a problem. My thighs and calves were muscled, but I'd trimmed down at least a size in my waist, probably two.

My fear of the fitting room had amped from uncomfortable to panic attack the last time Mom tried this shopping thing with me. Rationally, I could go in an enclosed space, try on pants, and come back out fully dressed. Irrationally, the anxiety raised my heart rate, and I felt barred in by expectations. People watched fitting rooms like runways.

Max squeezed my hand again. "We're almost done."

"I hate being on display."

"Should I pitch a fit?" he asked.

I shook my head. "I need to do this."

Mom put four pairs of jeans over my shoulder and escorted me to the back of the store. Just as I released Max's hand, Gina opened a stall door and walked out.

"Sadie." She followed our hands up Max's long body to a face she thought she recognized.

I watched her gasp, watched her knees nearly buckle. "Oh my God." She clutched her chest as if she was having a heart attack and vaulted backward into the attendant, who bumped into a rack of clothes. Both the attendant and the rack nose-dived into the floor. An explosion of clothes and headbands and socks and scarfs followed. Eight stall mirrors showed Gina's surprise and tackle from every angle.

"Oh shit. Oh shit," said the young store attendant. She dropped several more hangers full of clothes trying to find her balance.

"I'm sorry," Gina said.

Sonia and I flanked Gina while Max and Mom helped the attendant right the rack and retrieve the clothes from across the fitting room floor.

"I'm sorry. I'm so sorry," Gina repeated.

Whether it was to the attendant or to Max, I couldn't tell. The attendant waved her off as if she'd had quite enough Gina Adler in her day.

I watched the methodical way Sonia stroked Gina's arm. "We'll get it fixed, honey," she told Gina.

This girl had grown up on the couch in Sonia's living room, stretched out next to her lanky, beautiful, rambunctious boy. There must have been moments when she'd wondered if Trent and Gina would stay together. She'd even had Gina sit with the family during the funeral.

"It's okay," I told Gina as I helped her sit down on a bench.

Gina ducked her head. "I'm so embarrassed."

"Don't be. I had the same reaction."

I hadn't, but I thought it might make her feel better. No one contradicted me.

So far, today was a no-blame, extra-sympathy-for-Gina day.

After Max finished helping the attendant, I waved him over.

He hesitated, but approached. "Hi, Gina." I barely heard him.

"Your voice is better."

"It exists," he agreed.

"I'm so glad you're back," she said, and stood to hug him properly.

I found myself staring at a distorted version of an image I'd seen many times. Rewind the clock, and this was Trent and Gina. She must have known it, because she'd turned to catch my eye.

I didn't hold this embrace against her, and I let her know with a slight nod.

When she let go, she said, "We should all get together tonight. I could call Gray. We could go to the jetty or something."

"Um . . ." Max checked with me before he answered.

I opted out quickly, not wanting to press my luck. "I usually run."

"You can skip one night, right?" Gina asked. "Come on, I'd love to spend some time with you. Both of you. Hear about El Salvador."

There she was, with her constant invitations that led to constant apologies. I shrugged my shoulders, held up the jeans as if I needed to get to the stall, and said, "Maybe some other time."

She nodded in defeat. I'd refused enough invitations that she didn't seem surprised. Gina hugged Max again and gave me a sad little stare. "Sometime this summer? Please," she said to me.

My head moved up and down; the scar at my mouth twisted as I bit my lip. "Sometime." Thinking about the list, I threw her a bone. "Maybe for Pirates and Paintball."

"I'm sorry about the . . . you know." Max finger-puppeted her tackling the attendant.

"No, I'm sorry." Color rose in her cheeks. "Pirates and Paintball," she repeated. "Let's make it a plan."

Max massaged his neck. "If Sadie wants to," he rasped.

"I've been doing everything I can to get her out of that shell she lives in. Max, please remind her that she used to do stuff with us. Stuff like riding motorcycles—"

Sonia, who was listening, interrupted with an answer of her own. "And skipping school and going to the water park."

I wanted a sinkhole to open up and suck me into the bowels of the earth. Even Sonia McCall was trying to get me out of the house by suggesting something that had gotten me grounded for a month. I was pathetic.

Sonia touched my shoulder warmly and added, "The kids have a point. You really should have some fun this summer."

Well, on that note, it was time to end the conversation. I held up my jeans, walked straight into the dressing room, and collapsed onto the bench with my pile of denim.

"I love your bangs," Gina called over the wall.

In my head, I heard Trent. This time, *Hold on. Hold on. Hold on* came out like *Forgive her, Sadie May; you'll get her back.*

"I don't want to," I told him.

The voice in my head, whether it was Trent or my own conscience, knew the same Latin phrase I knew. *A posse ad esse.*

"Shut up," I whispered.

The voice wandered away, and I felt like I'd kicked a dog.

CHAPTER FOURTEEN

Some Emails to Max in El Salvador

From: sadiemaykingston@gmail.com

To: tothemax@thecenter.es

Date: September 13

Subject: Prayers

Max,

I know you're the praying sort, so if you don't mind, would you say one for me and Gray? For the first time, I am starting to believe we won't make it.

He came over yesterday and . . . I think he wanted to break up with me and couldn't figure out how. I just sat there. I honestly don't know whether to hold on or let go.

Sadie

From: sadiemaykingston@gmail.com

To: tothemax@thecenter.es

Date: September 15

Subject: Bad News

Max,

I went for a walk on Monday night and caught Gray and Gina on the beach together. She said he was drunk. He swore it didn't mean anything. She pleaded with me to understand it was an accident. (WTF? Is there such a thing as accidental groping?) He said he was sorry. She cried. They promised they never meant for anything to happen.

There wasn't much to say after that.

Sadie

From: sadiemaykingston@gmail.com

To: tothemax@thecenter.es

Date: September 18

Subject: No

Max,

I don't want you to beat him up. I just have to figure out what to do.

Sadie

From: sadiemaykingston@gmail.com
To: tothemax@thecenter.es
Date: September 20
Subject: Done-Done

Max,
I broke up with him.

                              Sadie

From: sadiemaykingston@gmail.com
To: tothemax@thecenter.es
Date: September 24
Subject: Theory

Max,
I can't believe you overnighted that card. It was the first time I
smiled in three days. Thank you.
    I have a theory on what happened.
    Step one: Change happens. (The wreck.)
    Step two: Pretend the change doesn't exist. (What wreck?)
    Step three: Get angry the other person can't be who they
used to be. (You're a wreck.)
    Step four: Create change. (Wreck this.)
    I wish I could hate them and mean it.

                              Sadie

From: sadiemaykingston@gmail.com

To: tothemax@thecenter.es

Date: September 30

Subject: RE: Theory

Max,

No, the worst part isn't that it was with Gina. That's awful. Sure. The worst part is this feels like it's my fault.

My dad's mom, Pazie, has this formal dining room, and it's so formal no one is allowed to use it. Some people have hearts like that, and I'm worried I'm becoming one of them. I feel myself shutting down, closing off, like I should tell people, "No, we don't use this heart anymore. It's too fragile."

It started with the crash. I held on to all these emotions and truths that I should have expressed, but I didn't know how to say what I needed to say. I thought that would ruin us. Well, silence ruined us too.

I'm not saying Gray and Gina are off the hook, but maybe some part of what happened between Gray and Gina happened because I put my heart in the formal dining room and told him (and her) he couldn't go in there.

I don't want this thing in my chest to beat me to death, but I also don't want to protect it so much that I never use it again.

Sadie

From: sadiemaykingston@gmail.com

To: tothemax@thecenter.es

Date: October 2

Subject: Pinkie swears

Max,

Yes, I'm a little bit better today. And I promise I will try to never put our friendship in the formal dining room. I can't lose you, too. I won't have anyone left.

Sadie

CHAPTER FIFTEEN

Mom banged on the fitting room door. "Sadie."

I opened it, and she slipped inside. She was always slipping behind my barriers.

"Oh, honey," she said when she saw me.

Oh, honey opened a floodgate. I'd changed many behaviors over the last year, but I rarely purged emotions for anyone. She sat, and I lay my head in her lap. "I'm sorry I made you do this," she said.

Sorry slid nicely into my broken places until I was able to sit up again. Mom held my face in her hands, thumbed away my rogue tears.

"I don't know why I'm crying," I said. "Why this is all so hard for me. Why everyone has to be my intervention. Jesus, even Sonia thinks I'm broken."

"I don't know either, baby doll."

"Mom . . . I don't want to be mad at them anymore. I know it was an accident, but when I see them, Gray or Gina, something tightens right here." I shoved my fingers into the place at the bottom of my rib cage. "Will that ever go away?"

My mother stroked my hair and gave me an honest answer. "I don't know."

"I hate hate."

"Me too, Sadie. Me too."

She didn't try to fix the hurt or offer trite expressions. My mother spoke with her arms, tightening them around my body, until my breathing returned to normal. I lingered there in her safety until my stomach settled enough so I could stand.

"What do you say we call it a day?" she said. Then she gathered up the jeans I never tried on and slipped out of the room.

I followed her example. She was at the counter, buying all four pair of jeans, so I darted toward the door and escaped. Max's hand found mine again, and he walked us away from the crowds. Back at the van, he opened my door for me and handed me a sack.

"You won't want it yet, but I want to be there when you do." Then he kissed my temple, a tiny peck, and walked around to the other side of the van.

I touched the place where his lips had been and looked at the sack. It was from a store where I used to shop. I peeked inside and saw Max's purchase.

A tank top.

Across the front was the popular "You Only Live Once" saying. Bold lines marked through all the words except *Live*. Cutting my eyes to the back row, I mouthed a polite thank-you.

"That baby blue will look awesome with your eyes," he said.

"Thank you."

Wear a tank top in public. It was first on my list.

Max's optimism concerned me. What if this thing that had grown between us was based on who he thought I might be someday rather than who I was? Even though he'd lost his brother, his progress looked like an ascent rather than a plateau. So far, I hadn't figured out how to accept the new story of my life. Should I shut down this hand-holding, heart-holding kindness before it heaped more heartache on us both?

I didn't want to.

I wanted to put on a tank top and walk in the sunshine with Max. All the way home, I imagined a world where I could.

When we pulled into the driveway, I surprised everyone by following Max into his house instead of mine. I didn't want to try on jeans or put away clothes or see my traitorous bird. I wanted company.

That was a good change.

We sat in each other's space, close enough that we shared a couch cushion. After a year apart, happiness was the comfort of being able to hug each other anytime we wanted. Sonia popped kettle corn and put on an old version of *Peter Pan*. We didn't watch much of the movie, but we did discuss all the films and television shows he'd missed over the past year. Everything from Woody Allen to Christopher Nolan to Wes Anderson to Aaron Sorkin. Max made a "Must Watch These Together" list. It would take ten years to get through all the titles he wanted to see with me. I liked that idea.

"You know my favorite show of all time—"

"Is *Buffy the Vampire Slayer*," he said.

"Did I tell you that before?" I asked, thinking about Big.

"No. I'm just observant."

Or was he covering up a little slip?

That thought made me switch the topic to his life in El Salvador. "Speaking of observant, I want to see all your El Salvador pictures."

After scrolling through a thousand photos, we ate BLTs at the kitchen counter and talked until his voice was gone and I didn't have much to say.

By six o'clock, a heaviness made our twosome a threesome. Without a word, Max led me into Trent's room, and we both curled up in his bed. Him on one side. Me against the wall. I was in a bed with my boyfriend, and we were both thinking about his brother. It wasn't romantic; it was exactly what I needed.

"I've been sleeping in here," Max said.

"I took a nap in here once while you were gone."

We tried to hold each other, but we were both stiff, unyielding. "You know why I sleep in here?" Max asked.

"No."

"This room is full of mysteries."

I rolled over and watched him. Max was flat on his back, hands squeezed into fists, eyes locked on the ceiling. He didn't blink. Didn't move.

"What do you mean?" I asked, and flopped on my back. Above me, a pattern of glow-in-the-dark star stickers shone. I focused in on them and listened.

Anger, and maybe . . . guilt, crept into Max's tone. "Like, there are pieces of him I didn't know or understand. We shared a frickin' bedroom wall. How did I miss . . ." He exhaled, but it was a beginning rather than an end. "When did he build that Lego temple-thing on the desk? Who gave him the card he kept between his mattress and box spring? Gina? Was it her? Was it you? Someone else? They loved him, whoever it was."

I didn't dare interrupt, but I inched my hand closer to him.

He continued. "What happened to his YOLO paddle? Where did he get that black leather jacket? We live in Florida, for God's sake. When would he need a leather jacket? And those damn tennis shoes with the toes in them, when did he stop wearing Scotts? Did you know he kept a journal? And did you know he ripped out more than half of it? Why? What was in there? God, I shouldn't have even looked at it."

Max had so many questions that his voice dissolved into scratching sounds rather than words. He rarely spoke in paragraphs, opting for clipped answers that saved his voice. I pieced together the last thing he said before he went silent. "He would bust my ass if he knew I went through his stuff."

I nodded a yes at the last comment, but really, I nodded at all of the questions. I knew some of the answers, but letting Max know I knew, when he didn't know, felt cruel. Still, I offered him the only truth I understood.

"I think maybe everyone is a mystery. Even the people we know really well. If I died"—he turned toward me, fear splashed across his reddened face, and latched our pinkies together—"and you went through my stuff, you'd have the same type of questions. Why I kept one thing but not another. What I was hiding and telling and hoping and believing. We all have that stuff, and it'll drive you crazy if you fixate on it. I know. In a different way, I've been doing the same thing with Gina and Gray. Acting as if answers will change feelings. I'm not sure it works that way."

"Sadie?"

"Yeah."

His face relaxed into a near-smile. "Tell me something you've never told me."

I laced my hands behind my head and relaxed.

"I made Trent that Lego temple-thing as a thank-you for helping me study for the SAT. It's supposed to be Machu Picchu. We were planning a trip someday."

Max nodded. "Yeah, he loved explorers. Even the brutal ones like Ponce."

"He didn't love Ponce for Ponce. He loved Ponce because he loved the Fountain of Youth. And he loved the Fountain of Youth because"—my eyes swelled with tears and I ground my teeth into my final words—"he was scared of dying."

Max pulled me to his chest and found the strength for a few more words. "I'll tell you something I've never told you. In the end, he wasn't scared."

"How do you know?"

"Because I was there."

CHAPTER SIXTEEN

We took a long nap and I woke up around ten. When I opened my eyes, I gave Max a lazy look and he threw a thumb toward the window, toward our dock. "You . . . want to sit out—"

I wondered how long he'd been awake.

"Yeah. Let me check in with Mom and Dad first. They'll be worried," I said, thinking I really wanted to brush the nap-fur off my teeth.

Max's cheek quivered. An almost-smile that I almost missed. For all the hard stuff we'd talked about today, that smile was like an eraser. I loved it. We walked to my deck together, and he took a seat on the edge of an Adirondack chair as if to say, *I'll wait right here.*

I waved. My attempt at a wordless *I'll be right back.*

He nodded.

After all those emails, we could speak without words.

The door was unlocked and lights were on in the kitchen. I stopped by and found Mom and Dad in some sort of hug.

Teasingly, I shielded my eyes. "I'm home. I'm home."

Dad kissed Mom on the tip of her nose. I should have been fifty shades of grossed out by my parents, but they'd always been this way. It was sweet when you considered that many of my classmates' parents stayed married because they had children and expensive mortgages. My mom and dad liked each other. From what I could tell, happiness was getting stuck with someone and never feeling stuck.

Are you okay? Mom asked with her eyes.

Better, I said, also without words. I was pretty decent at nonverbals tonight.

"I'm going down to the dock," I announced.

"No run?" Mom asked.

"Not tonight," I answered. No run. No list. No Latin phrases. No worries about Big. I'd had enough of those today.

Mom licked some frosting off a spreader, acted casual, too casual, and said, "Max still with you?"

"Yeah."

My parents *wanted* to ask: Do you swear you're okay? Should we call Dr. Glasson? You know you can talk to us if you need to? They didn't ask or say any of those things; instead, they psychoanalyzed me from three feet away. Their eyes were piercing.

So I smiled at them.

And it worked.

The atmosphere lightened considerably. Mom offered me icing off a fingertip—buttercream heaven—and trusted my silence. No more *Oh, honeys* tonight.

After a full sixty seconds with my toothbrush, I darted toward the back door. Dad called at me, "Family movie sometime soon."

"Sure," I agreed as always.

"Tell Max to join us."

I smiled again. "I will."

"Honey . . ."

"I know, Mom. Love you too."

"Stay out late," Dad suggested.

The Social Experiments were finally working to my advantage.

Back on the deck, I apologized to Max for taking so long inside. "I interrupted my parents having sex."

"Seriously?"

"No, but they were up to something."

"My parents were like that too," he said.

"Were?" I asked, thinking they'd moved around the world to fix crap like that.

"Sometimes they're fine. Sometimes they're not."

I couldn't imagine the McCalls in separate houses or lives, but I still asked, "You're not worried about them, are you?"

"No. I think they grieve differently. Dad needs to move. Mom needs to sit and cry."

"What do you need?" I asked.

"To be able to remember him."

"Me too. Sometimes I still talk to him," I said, thinking if anyone understood, it would be Max.

"I do that." Max hooked an arm around me. "Did I ever tell you that he used to wake me up in the middle of the night?"

"No."

But he'd done that to me, too. *Peck. Peck. Peck.* On my window. *Sadie May . . .*

"We'd walk to Waffle House. He'd eat pancakes and play the jukebox. That's how we learned all those old songs."

"He never told me that."

"It was our thing."

"We always biked to the jetty on my birthday," I told him.

"Yeah, I know."

"You can remember him anytime you want with me," I offered.

He kissed my forehead and thanked me.

Down at the dock, we hung our feet over the bay and listened to the inky water lap against the posts beneath us. There was salt in the wind and moonlight on the water. Usually, when I breathed in this view, I was not small. I was part of something that covered two-thirds of the world.

Not tonight. I was a dust mote on a universe-size stage.

I realized, sitting there next to Max, that I didn't want to shrink the world so it would fit me better; I wanted to expand. That really, that's what Fletcher and I had been working on all year. Even though I was so damn slow about it.

"Star Time?" Max asked.

"Please," I answered.

Star Time was a Trent original. We'd all be hanging out, chatty as blue-haired ladies in a beauty shop, and he'd yell, "Star Time!"

That meant we should give ourselves to nature and shut up. Trent went balls-to-the-wall all day, but he was a big believer in listening to the world's little moments at night. Wherever we were on his parents' boat, we'd lie back, quiet as little shadows, and look for poetry in the night sky.

I thought I'd already found some. Now, if I could only find the strength to hold on to it.

In unison, Max and I reclined on the wooden planks. They were splintery and full of uneven places and raised screws, but so cozy and familiar, I could have taken another nap. I laced my hands over my belly button, and Max did the same.

"I like that one." Max pointed at the space above the Big Dipper.

"Cassiopeia?"

"Sure," he said.

He didn't care which constellation I picked. Picking out stars was like picking out snowflakes. It was difficult to tell if we'd chosen the same ones, but they were all good choices.

"Cassiopeia was a queen," I said.

He took his eyes off the sky. "Like you."

"Um, not exactly, Romeo, since she went around boasting

about her unrivaled beauty."

He laughed. "That *does* sound like you, but . . ." He turned back to the sky. "You should boast about your beauty."

"Max." I didn't mean to sound so condescending, but it came out that way before I could correct my tone.

"I'm not joking," he said.

"I don't even know how you can look at me when I look like this, much less bring beauty into it."

His mouth opened in an O, surprised. "Look like what? Sadie, you look just like you always have to me."

"Except with these." I pointed to Idaho and Nameless.

"That's not what I see."

"It feels like that's what everyone's looking at."

He huffed. "God, I'd like to kick Gray Garrison in the nads." He sat up and forced me to do the same. His hands cupped my face and he locked eyes with me. "Look at me."

We were inches apart. There was nowhere else to look.

"Your face is beautiful, but I'm not some shallow asshole who falls in love with a face. You hear me?"

That rasp in his voice was perfect.

I braved an answer. "Yes."

"Sadie, you could go through a million windows and nothing would change."

He leaned forward.

Our noses touched.

I thought about his lips.

I imagined he'd close his eyes soon, but he didn't.

His head tilted—a clear invitation—lingering just far enough away that I still had a choice. Then, he moved his hand to my hip and part of me that had been asleep for a long time woke up. I made my choice.

A kiss can be a kiss or it can be an event.

I have cared about Max McCall all my life. Never like *this*, but since we were three and nine and twelve and fifteen and this past year and everywhere in between. Friends had become friends who became more than friends.

"I couldn't see you when we were kids," I said when there was finally room to speak.

He tucked a tangle of blond hair behind my ear. "We were kids." Max sat up, pulling me with him.

"Yeah, but you were also Trent's little brother."

"I still am, Sadie." Hesitation appeared, and I leaned back as he said, "I look like him."

"You also look like you," I told him.

He kissed me again.

When we were done and watching the stars again, Max scratched out a few words. "The stars are noisy tonight."

They were. A long time went by in comfortable silence. I counted a hundred stars more than once, and looked for patterns in the darkness rather than in the light.

Peace hid from me this year, and I'd searched for it at Metal Pete's, in therapy sessions, in long runs on the beach, and hours of Star Time. I hadn't found it hiding among that dark, black sea of sparkles or anywhere else. But tonight, in the gentleness of my friend stretched out next to me, breathing in and out so rhythmically that he sounded like breaking waves, it felt within reach again.

After a lifetime of life-by-group, followed by a time of isolation, it was nice to have someone to be quiet with.

I stole a look, and because he was so focused on the sky, I stole a few more.

Max. Long, tan, a tiny bit of skin showing at his hips from the way he'd stretched back out. He wore a glazed look of wonder that was childlike and sweet and handsome, and he went a long time without blinking. Just like he'd done in Trent's bed. I liked that about him. The intensity he gave to life.

How did you end up being the guy lying next to me?

We'd been silent for so long, I couldn't tell the difference between a question I asked in my head and one I asked aloud. I was mortified when he responded.

"Gray doesn't speak star."

I begged the darkness to have mercy and beam me up; my face felt hot as a fever.

Max made nothing of my comment or his; he didn't even roll his eyes to the side to check on me. I let his ease become mine. I'd been doing that a lot lately.

"What are the stars telling you?" I asked.

Max pushed up on his elbows and pretended to strain his ear toward the sky. "They say . . . They say . . . you're allowed to forgive yourself."

I rolled sideways . . . and he did the same.

"For what?" I asked.

"Living."

"I'm not very good at that," I admitted.

"Well, you just kissed someone without flinching. Maybe you're getting better."

"Maybe it's just you."

He didn't argue.

CHAPTER SEVENTEEN

Some Emails to Max in El Salvador

From: sadiemaykingston@gmail.com

To: tothemax@thecenter.es

Date: October 27

Subject: Game

Max,

Would you like to play a game? Gray and I used to obsess over one called Tell Me Something You've Never Told Me. The rules are as simple as they sound. I'll go first.

I've been skinny-dipping.

If you'd like to play, all you have to do is tell me something you've never told me.

Sadie

From: sadiemaykingston@gmail.com
To: tothemax@thecenter.es
Date: October 29
Subject: pirate confessions

Just last week, Fletcher said two of the most powerful words in the universe are "Me too." I believe him. Ha. Ha. At least where skinny-dipping is concerned. I didn't know you had a thing with Candace.

Next Tell Me Something You've Never Told Me:

The very first year of Pirates and Paintball, I'm the one who shot Trent. Do you remember that he was convinced it was Callahan?

Your turn!

                                        Sadie

From: sadiemaykingston@gmail.com
To: tothemax@thecenter.es
Date: November 4
Subject: Callahan

Max,
Yeah, Trent and Callahan were pretty tight. Have you heard from him at all? We've texted a few times. Not that long ago he asked if I wanted to ride motorcycles, but I told him I wasn't up for it yet.

Which leads me to *Something I've Never Told You*:

Trent and I used to borrow Callahan's motorcycle and go riding in the country.

Next?

Sadie

From: sadiemaykingston@gmail.com

To: tothemax@thecenter.es

Date: November 5

Subject: Hilarious

Max,

That's hilarious. Do you miss her?

Also, I'm pretty sure Callahan isn't hitting on me. I'm not his type. I'm not really anyone's type anymore. He knew Trent and I used to borrow the motorcycle and wanted to offer something I loved. Callahan's a great guy. I really should text him.

Something I've Never Told You:

I tried to drive to the Fountain of Youth this week. And by tried, I mean I got in my parents' car and put it in reverse. I rolled three feet.

Tell Me Something.

Sadie

From: sadiemaykingston@gmail.com

To: tothemax@thecenter.es

Date: November 12

Subject: best laid plans

Max,

I don't know why the fountain is so important. Maybe because Trent and I wanted to go exploring when we were kids. Maybe because it was the last thing we made plans to do. Maybe because it represents a type of healing, and I could use some of that. I have to find a way to go.

What you said about me being someone's type was generous.

With that in mind, here's a serious Tell Me Something:

I'm afraid I'll never feel desirable again. Afraid I'll never kiss someone without them flinching. And then I'll flinch and back away. Action. Reaction. I can predict it perfectly. My life seems like a constant backpedal.

Your turn. (It doesn't have to be serious.)

Sadie

From: sadiemaykingston@gmail.com

To: tothemax@thecenter.es

Date: November 13

Subject: Lies

Max,

That can't be your Tell Me Something.

Tell Me Somethings have to be true.

Plus, you sound like my mom. That inner-beauty thing is the first cousin of "You're pretty on the inside." I'm not saying that's what you meant, I'm only saying no girl wants to be in the *pretty on the inside* camp.

My new Tell Me Something:

I need to tell Gina and Gray something, but I don't know how. They've made some wrong assumptions, and I feel trapped between defending myself and telling the truth. Do you think there's such a thing as a good lie?

Yours?

Sadie

From: sadiemaykingston@gmail.com
To: tothemax@thecenter.es
Date: November 20
Subject: RE: US?

Max,

Whoa, your Tell Me Something caught me off guard. Do you mean *us* as *a couple*?

If so, Max, you're so sweet to try making me feel desirable, but you don't have to do that. (Guess you do believe in good lies. 😊) You live there, and I live here. *Us* is a horrible idea.

Your emails are more than enough. More than I ever expected.

However, my Tell Me Something is:

If you weren't there, and I weren't here . . . If I weren't me . . . but you were still you, I would be interested in letting you like-like me.

Next?

Sadie

CHAPTER EIGHTEEN

The first half of the week dripped by like an old faucet. Gina reached out by email. Gray texted. Both wanted us all to attend Pirates and Paintball.

I ignored the communications, which only made them send more.

They weren't the only ones who brought it up. Thursday morning, Max was on the back deck waiting for me. He walked me to the mailbox.

"Pretty sure the mail runs later in the day," he said. "Like after the sun comes up."

What did that mean? I didn't take the bait, if that's what it was.

"I forgot to check it yesterday."

"Expecting love letters?" he asked playfully.

If this was an open door, I played it halfway in, halfway out. "Are you writing me one?"

"Maybe."

Then he elbowed me and winked. I tasted the orange juice I'd just downed in the kitchen, and swallowed hard.

"We're past our letter-writing days," I said suggestively.

"I'll keep that in mind for the future. So, besides the mailbox, where is it you run off to in the mornings?" Max asked.

I shied away from telling him about Metal Pete's. It was something I hadn't exactly disclosed in my emails, and I worried he wouldn't understand my obsession.

"Uh . . ."

His eyes rolled up and away. His jaw set and he asked, "Do you go sit with Gray?"

"No!" I said quickly. "I'll show you, but no commentary. Okay?"

"I'd rather know than wonder."

I retrieved two helmets from the garage, and we climbed on the Spree.

"Did you choose this instead of a car because of riding motorcycles with Trent?" he asked as we pulled into Jenni's parking lot at the Donut Barista.

"No. Maybe. I never thought of that."

"Any luck driving?" he asked.

"Nope."

"You'll get it," he said as we walked up to the barista shack.

"Ooh, I've been waiting for an introduction," Jenni said,

leaning out the window.

"Jenni, this is Max."

"As in Maximilian," she cooed, making Max blush.

"As in Maxwell, ma'am," he said.

"Well, what does Maxwell love to drink?"

He let me choose for him. I ordered the usual plus a Pacho Nuevo black coffee blend and two crullers.

"Well done," he said as Jenni left to prepare our food. "So . . . you talk about me to your barista?" His cheeks were as pink as the sunset.

"Yes. And I call you Maximilian."

We left Jenni's loaded down with sugar and caffeine. I wagered we'd need both for Max's first Salvage Yard experience. Lord, I hated to break his smile.

When we rolled into Metal Pete's, Max had questions he didn't ask. I watched the way his eyes narrowed and he surveyed the rows of cars. Headlight trotted out to greet me, and I introduced them.

There is something about dogs. They understand. Better than most humans. Headlight nuzzled Max with the best of her affection. Pre-love for the trip to the Yaris.

We walked to the office. Metal Pete wasn't there, so I left a note on the door and explained to Max that this old yard was my sanctuary.

"You come here every day?" Max asked, sipping the coffee.

"Most of them."

"What do you do?"

"Well, I talk to Metal Pete, look for cars, and . . . I sit by the Yaris."

"Trent's Yaris." His voice rose in surprise.

"Yeah."

"Jesus."

"I know it's weird."

"It's . . . unexpected," he said carefully.

"I look for courage here."

Max's eyes roamed over the lot around us. He took in the decaying metal field and said, "And you find it?"

"I find something."

I thought he was disgusted with the idea, but he took a doughnut from the bag, held it firmly between his teeth, and said, "Show me," as he chomped down.

Headlight walked between us as we made our way to the row where the Yaris lived.

"This place is like a cemetery."

"No. In a cemetery everything is final. This place is like a huge spare-parts store." I pointed to a totaled Camaro. "See. Those side mirrors, the tires, the steering wheel, maybe the bucket seats, plus who-knows-what under the hood: all of it's salvageable."

"Is there stuff missing from the Yaris?" Max asked.

"You'll see."

When we got to Trent's car, Max walked around it several times. I didn't disturb him. He needed this moment the same as I'd needed mine. Headlight trailed behind him, always within petting distance. Max opened the door to what was once his seat. It creaked angrily, but he and Headlight crawled inside and sat on the floor, since the backseat was gone. It must have been ninety degrees in there, but he showed no signs of moving.

I slipped down the row so he could cry in peace. While I waited, I rewrote the list in the dust on the hood of an old Buick.

1. Wear a tank top in public
2. Walk the line at graduation
3. Forgive Gina and Gray. And tell them the truth.
4. Stop following. Start leading.
5. Drive a car again
6. Visit the Fountain of Youth

As I stared at those six lines, I realized something I hadn't noticed on the beach. Seven was now six. I had kissed someone without flinching. The list, the impossible list, wasn't impossible.

Someone else might laugh at my revelation. Let them laugh. Taking a real step forward in life was frickin' hard.

For the first time in a year, I was proud of myself.

I stretched my arms wide into the crystal-blue sky that even this far from the ocean smelled like salt, and thanked God for vitamin D and possibilities. Then, I ripped off my long-sleeve shirt and danced around like an idiot while the courage lasted.

Three claps stopped me dancing.

I whipped around to see Max crawling out of the Yaris wearing a red face and a smile. Embarrassed that I was dancing in the salvage yard and that my boyfriend had caught me, I slipped my shirt back on, but I kept my grin in place.

He met me halfway, near the Buick.

"Hey, Sadie, that was a tank top."

"Yeah, it was."

Glancing over at the list, he ran his finger through number one.

"I'm not sure it counts since I didn't know you were watching," I said.

"It's a beginning."

"Did you have a new beginning?" I asked, indicating the Yaris.

"Nah, I had an end."

I took his hand and stopped him from walking down the aisle. He lifted the fedora off my head and held it against my back as he hugged me. Our chests rose and fell until they were in harmony.

Our hearts faced each other.

We danced, standing still.

Finally, he said, "We lived."

"Exactly."

Max put his wet cheek next to mine. "That's why you come here," he said.

"That's why I come here," I repeated.

"I like the way you think, Kingston."

"I like the way you understand, McCall."

On our way to the Spree, I stopped in the office. Metal Pete was back. He thanked me for the coffee and doughnuts and apologized for being in the house when I got here.

"I've got a favor to ask you," I said.

"Okay. Shoot."

The words propelled out of me of their own accord. "Will you help me drive again?" I asked.

Metal Pete knocked his knuckles against the desk in triumph and said, "Ah, hell, kid, I'll even throw in a car."

"None of these cars run," I teased.

"Well, beggars can't be choosers."

CHAPTER NINETEEN

Hours later, the universe jumped on board my anti-pity party and shoved life at me in the form of my mother.

She met me at the door with another envelope.

The envelope went in my pocket—to be dealt with the moment I got out of the living room.

"So," Mom began. "I've talked to the McCalls, the Adlers, and the Garrisons and . . ."

I anticipated what she was going to say: Pirates and Paintball.

". . . and everyone agrees we should resume the tradition of attending Pirates and Paintball," she continued.

Before the accident, the Pirates and Paintball game was an annual thing our four families attended together. Sonia's former hospital sponsored the community game, and we'd been

participating for years. Who wouldn't? Cosplayed pirate paintball was a win from every angle. (Unless you'd developed a
sudden hatred for crowds.) Over time, we stretched the Saturday morning game into a full weekend. On the Friday before,
the fourteen of us, or fifteen, if Gray's sister, Maggie, was on
leave, piled onto the McCalls' boat with our gear and headed
toward a campground near the little island where it was played.
After we prevailed as paintball victors, we stuck around to shell
and fish and camp, wasting away the weekend in proper beach-
bum fashion.

"Mom."

She held up her hand, not letting me speak. "We haven't
gone anywhere as a family in a long time." She threw in some
bait. "At least this would be with Max."

I tossed back some truth. "And Gray and Gina."

Mom nodded. "Maybe it would be an opportunity to patch
some things up."

"We're not a quilt."

She'd armed herself with more reasons, and she kept them
coming like balls at the batting cage. "You love paintball. And
camping. And Dad insists you get out more, and this will be so
good to do together before—"

"Mom, I'm in." I rode the wave of this morning's success:
"And, I'm going to kick everyone's asses at paintball."

Her high-five hand shot up. I tagged it hard, but not too hard.

"You do that," Mom said, not even bothering to warn me
about language.

I darted off to my room with the new envelope, before she started singing "Kumbaya." Big's huge eyes followed me from my bed to my dressing chair to the closet.

"What are *you* looking at, Big Mouth?" I asked the ostrich.

I opened the letter and braced myself for regurgitated words. This one was from my freshman year.

```
Gina and I convinced Trent, Gray, and Max to
skip school and go to the water park. Best idea
ever.
—From a friend who cares
```

Just last week, Sonia brought up this very occasion in the dressing room.

I leaned back onto my bed.

A friend who cares? Sonia would never call herself a friend; she was a parent.

But Gina would. And she'd surely heard Sonia's reference.

The *friend* hadn't shown up in the first note, but had in the second, and now he or she claimed to be a *caring* individual. Awesome. Someone had been poorly trained in the rules of affection. Regardless, the letters had a progression to them. The first one, skinny-dipping, was about Trent and me. The second one, bridge-jumping, was with Gray. This third one was about all five of us. The five of us hadn't been together all that often.

Did that mean anything?

Also, Gina and I weren't mentioned in a specific memory, except within this group one. Did that implicate her?

I thought back through that day and searched for clues.

I was the first to notice the sun was too perfect for school. The sidewalk beside Coast Memorial High School led to boredom and monotony on such a fabulous day.

"You guys, I can't . . ."

"Can't what?" Trent said.

"Be here. Look at this day. It's practically a crime to be inside."

Trent and Gina paused. We never skipped school, which meant we could. Our faithful obedience to the system meant we'd earned some flextime.

Gina scrunched her forehead, curious enough to listen. "What are you thinking, Sade?"

"It's a perfect day to race down the waterslides at Cannon Balls."

Gina looked at Trent, who was already nodding.

"Yes indeed, Sadie May. You have said a true thing, and we have an obligation to follow you."

"What are you? Yoda?" Gray asked as he mocked Trent's words.

Max was the only one still focused on school.

"If you skip, you still have to pick me up," he told Trent.

Trent tapped the top of the Yaris, excited about a prison break. "You don't want to come with?"

Max's eyebrows lifted in surprise. "I'm invited?"

"What can I say? I'm feeling generous," Trent boasted, sticking out his chest.

Max didn't look comfortable going to Cannon Balls as a fifth wheel, so I threw an arm around his shoulder and coaxed him into going along with our stupid idea. "Come on. It'll be fun to have you along," I told him.

That was all it took. He climbed in the backseat while Gina and Gray—who always carpooled from their side of town—grabbed their always-ready beach bags and left his mom's van in the parking lot. Five of us in the Yaris were a snug fit, but we couldn't skip school in a mom-mobile.

"You got trunks on you, little bro?" Trent asked.

"I can roll," Max said. "I'm calling it now: Mom will find out about this."

Trent bent his arm into the backseat and patted Max's knee. "She won't find out unless you tell her."

"Lips are zipped," Max promised.

We arrived at Cannon Balls, and as usual, Max trailed along two steps behind the four of us. I caught his eye, and beckoned him forward. He sped up quickly then. The day shaped up even more perfectly when the five of us walked to the ticket booth to pay and a recent Coast Memorial alum, Winter Halson, waved us through without charge. Even the universe didn't want us inside today.

Trent leaned through the window and punched Winter on the arm. "Thanks, man."

"Anything for a brother," Winter said.

Trent had a talent for making brothers.

"You're ballsy, McCall," Winter called after us.

"Sadie May gets the cred for this one," Trent yelled back, and kissed Gina on the cheek.

An hour later, Max and I were at the top of the speed tubes. He gave me a "Race you" challenge, and I nodded, eyes blazing. So far, I'd beaten Trent, Gray, and Gina to the bottom. Four for four sounded good to me, but Max was in total beast mode.

Just before we hurled ourselves down the plastic chutes, his expression softened, and he said, "Thanks for inviting me today."

I did what anyone in my position would have done. I pushed off from the top ahead of him and screamed, "No worries!" as I dropped and spun.

The words echoed around me. The water propelled me forward, faster, faster, faster into my perfect day. I was sure I would win.

Dammit if Max didn't emerge two seconds ahead of me. Dammit squared. He shot so far out he crashed into a woman wading across the pool to the lazy-river entrance. A Cannon Balls employee blew her whistle.

"Sorry, ma'am," Max said without looking, flipping his hair back and spewing droplets everywhere. Then he whipped around to me and smirked. "Creamed you, Kingston."

Technically, he'd creamed Sonia McCall, his mother, since she was the lady he'd mowed down into the cement bottom of the pool.

Sonia came to her full senses well before Max realized his mistake.

"Maxwell Lincoln McCall, why aren't you in school?"

Whoa. Full name.

"Because it—uh . . . I mean," he stuttered. "It was practically a crime to be inside, Mom," Max said very tentatively, and glanced at me for support.

I winked at Max again behind Sonia's back. Ballsy, McCall, I heard Winter Halson's voice in my head.

Sonia turned, her eyes boring into mine. The cobra hood of her inner snake swelled and stood on end as she prepared to strike. "Sa-die."

I flipped up my hand in a wave. "It really is a perfect day for Cannon Balls," I said.

Tara Kingston would have been proud of the look Sonia shot me. I shriveled appropriately, but something in me found this downright comical. Come on, what were the odds? I got the feeling Sonia agreed with me, but on the very principles of being a parent, plus a card-carrying adult, had to pretend otherwise. After all, she and Mr. McCall had jobs. We weren't the only ones skipping obligations.

"Where's your brother?" she growled at Max.

Max pointed at the huge clock above the cantina. "I'm guessing in language arts. Maybe psychology."

Admirable. Trent would have thrown him to the wolves.

That answer wouldn't have held even if Trent and Gina hadn't shot out of the tubes at the same time, to more whistles of annoyance from the Cannon Balls staff. Sonia wiped the chlorine from her eyes again and waded out of the pool. We followed her like little ducks, partly because we had to, and partly so the whistle-blowing employee would chill the freak out.

Mr. McCall sat up from his chair—after an apparent nap—and

said, "Hey, Max," before he registered Max was not where Max was supposed to be.

"Hey, Dad."

"Where's Gray?" Sonia's head snapped back and forth. "You four, don't even attempt to lie to me. Where one of you goes, the rest of you follow."

Gray's timing was impeccable. He arrived as if on cue, licking an orange Push-Up pop. He tucked it behind his back and donned his best smile. "Hey, Mrs. McCall."

Sonia had us out of Cannon Balls and back in school within the hour. We spent a few weeks with our asses in slings—no car privileges, no dates—but no one could convince any of us it wasn't the best morning of the year. Absolutely epic.

I mean, really, who else would that happen to?

That was the whole memory.

Which meant I was still clueless. Except for the increasing certainty that Max, Gray, or Gina must be my anonymous *friend who cares*. Had Max returned from the salvage yard and typed this note while I dropped a library book in the bin for Mom? He'd had time, and reason. After all, he'd read the list on the Buick, knew I was attempting to resurrect the old me. Totally possible. I examined the chronology again.

Between the arrival of the first two notes, Gray had told me he still loved me, Max had come back from El Salvador, and Gina had apologized again. Between the second two, I'd confronted Gray, melted down in the dressing room with Gina, and amped things up with Max. Of everyone, Gina was the one acting the least suspicious.

Which meant . . . absolutely nothing.

Shit, what a mess. Was I supposed to do some big Eeny, Meeny, Miny, Moe game? Stake out my mailbox? Wait for someone to confess rather than accuse the wrong person?

It wouldn't have bothered me so badly if someone hadn't gone through Big to do this. Big wasn't exactly my diary, but some of the things *were* personal. They were definitely things I should have the choice to share or withhold—like the Sharpie stuff.

These messages, regardless of their intent, were a tour of memories from a different life.

That part was almost nice.

Almost.

CHAPTER TWENTY

Some Emails to Max in El Salvador

From: sadiemaykingston@gmail.com

To: tothemax@thecenter.es

Date: January 3

Subject: Big Explanations

Max,

I'm sitting in the doctor's office, waiting for them to call my name. I probably have plenty of time to finish how I started putting stuff into Big.

Part One: Obtaining Big.

I would never have started if your brother hadn't decided to win the world's ugliest stuffed animal as a gift for my twelfth birthday. He pointed to it behind the counter of the arcade.

"That one. That blue ostrich there beside the green pig. That's the one we're all going to win you, Sadie May."

It cost 1,800 tickets. I repeat, 1,800 tickets.

Gray added the stipulation that we must win all the tickets playing Skee-Ball. What a ruckus. You would have thought we were competing in the World Series with the way we jumped around and screamed. By the time we hit 1,500 tickets, the ticket-counter guy was in on it with us. It was a slow night, and we were the best action he'd had. I can't remember which of the guys starting calling the bird Big, but it stuck immediately.

Gray wanted to be the one who won the final tickets, so Gina and I stopped playing and watched as the final total rose to 1,800. In the excitement, Gray picked me up and kissed my cheek. I turned pink, as if he'd slipped me some tongue. But we weren't *there* yet. He was thirteen; I was twelve. Kissing was ascending Everest.

In light of how I've felt lately, I can look back and understand what made it an Everest sort of moment. I felt wanted. You know what I mean? That peck on the cheek wasn't a peck; it was a declaration that he wanted to kiss me.

Anyway, we walked out of the Family Fun Center five minutes after 8:00 with the world's ugliest Big.

Part Two: Stuffing Big.

Mom took us to a Chinese buffet and we grubbed up and told her all about Big. She pointed out that my new prize had a tiny hole in his belly. In her opinion, we'd spent, like, eighty dollars on something that wasn't worth anything.

As soon as I stopped smiling, Trent took the fortune out of his cookie, rolled it up, and stuck it inside the hole.

"Now, you know there's good stuff in there," he said.

God, he always had goofy ideas, didn't he?

Everyone else shoved in fortunes as Gina and Mom sang "Happy Birthday."

That's how it started.

Sadie

From: sadiemaykingston@gmail.com
To: tothemax@thecenter.es
Date: January 12
Subject: Stuck on a feeling

Max,

No, Big's not full yet. The papers are mostly small, and I don't write everything down. Just little memories and things I'm afraid I'll forget.

Fletcher says I tell Big the things I should tell friends—that my stuffed animal has become a defense mechanism. He suggested that Big allows me to withdraw and that the memories in him are uniquely tied to me, Gray, Trent, and Gina.

He wants me to either (a) make up with Gray and Gina, or (b) find an activity that introduces me to new people. And he thinks I need to get rid of Big.

I don't want new friends. I want my old friends to act like my old friends.

Which is a double standard.

I'd have to act like the old me again, and I don't think I can.

Sadie

CHAPTER TWENTY-ONE

Pirates and Paintball marched steadily in my direction. One week, three days, tomorrow. I tried to put the event in the back of my mind, which meant I thought about it constantly. The game offered a nice distraction from the forthcoming anniversary and my empty mailbox, which I had staked out two of those nights to no avail. Maybe I'd spooked the sender.

Every evening, I racked up more miles on the sand than with my driving lessons at Metal Pete's. Gina sent texts. I answered every single one. I wrote the list obsessively, longing to find something to eliminate—to hold on to some form of progress.

Six. I was stuck at six. Well, five, if I got half a point for sitting in a car and half a point for Max seeing me in a tank top.

Fletcher, whom I'd seen last week, assured me it did.

We'd spent most of our entire fifty minutes talking about Max's return and Gray's "I still love you."

"I'm assuming Gray's confession confused you," Fletcher had said.

"No. It pissed me off. If he still loved me, he'd look at me."

"Have you asked Gray why he can't look at you?"

Fletcher always pushed me away from assumptions and toward clarity, which I found annoying.

I'd opted for humor instead of an answer. "Um, I'm pretty sure I know, Fletcher. These scars can sing karaoke by themselves."

"Max looks at you?" Fletcher said.

"So far," I'd agreed.

Max was looking at me now. Smiling.

I lay on his bed reading a book while he tried route after route to the top of the climbing wall.

The book was a decoy. I loved watching him climb.

This had become a little routine of ours. After my run, I showered and came over. Sonia and Mr. McCall didn't mind as long as we kept the bedroom door open, and my parents didn't care as long as Sonia and Mr. McCall were home. There were ways around such things, but for now, I happily followed the rules. Intimacy, the kind that involved fewer clothes, and more scars, still unnerved me.

"You're just so"—I set the book down and searched for a word—"graceful."

He executed a move that would have sent me to the crash

mat, hung his head back, and looked at me upside down. "None of it feels graceful," he complained with a grunt.

Swinging his body back and forth, he leaped for a hold and missed. He fell and bounced on the mat. "See?"

Despite the fall, he was a dancer on a vertical floor. Every move looked effortless. His core twisted this way and that as he found new foot- and handholds.

Two falls later, he slapped the mat and massaged his swollen forearms. "Your turn," he said.

"Nope."

I had yet to try this intimidating thing he loved. There were enough things in life that made me feel weak; why add another? My nose went back in the book, and Max went back to the wall.

I read fifteen more pages.

I heard him coming before I felt him land next to me. Won over, I scooted closer and put my hand in his hair without moving my book from between us. If this was a real attempt to make a move, it wasn't particularly sexy. "Thank you," I said.

"For tackling you? For disturbing your book? For being one of those annoying guys who wants more attention?" he teased.

"Yes, yes, and it's not annoying."

"Good, because I like this much better than email."

I kissed the top of his nose. "True. Can't do that in an email."

He closed the gap between us. "Can't do this, either." His hand slid up the back of my shirt; his lips met mine.

To keep things from going any further, I hopped up and approached the climbing wall.

"Where do I start?" I asked.

Max assembled a pillow pile and flopped back into some comfort. Good-naturedly, he changed gears. "Anywhere you want. Remember, bouldering is a game of inches."

"Is that a challenge, McCall?" I asked.

"You kidding?" Max shifted around to watch what I figured would be a very short show. "You'll top out." He held one finger in the air to say, *On the first time.*

That wasn't going to happen, but I liked his confidence.

I chalked my hands the way he always did, found two deep handholds near the bottom, and pulled up on the wall.

"Nice," he said.

I wasn't graceful like him, but I wasn't awful. Each move was a victory. You never feel the weight of your own body until you have to hold it all with your fingertips. Fatigue slayed me two moves later; I froze, unable to coerce my right arm to let go and grab the next hold.

"Get that red one," Max said.

"I can't."

One iota of motion, and I'd fall. Instead of trying, I clung there, as if I were fifty feet in the air instead of five. The clinging surprised me. I had the energy to hold on, but not to advance.

"One more push, and you can rest," Max whispered.

Four inches. My pinkie stretched toward the hold. "Come on, body. Come on," I said.

No matter how I insisted, my hands refused to listen. My fingers ached from their crimped grip; my legs quivered beneath me. In the end, I fell off and landed on the mat.

"Really good," Max said.

"Yeah." I gave him my best fake nod. "That part where I got stuck was transcendent."

"No worries. All my climbs ended that way in the beginning."

Massaging the pads on my raw palms, I asked, "What happened to change that?"

"I fell, and it didn't kill me. So I decided that if I was going to fall, I might as well fall moving up."

What he said seemed to have more to do with my recent decision to move forward with the list than the climb I'd just attempted. Truth gets tucked into the strangest places.

"Wanna try again?" he asked.

I did. I wanted to try until I could do every climb on this wall. But not right now. I had another plan.

"Hey, how do you feel about a Waffle House run?" I asked, one eyebrow in a deviant arch.

"Love it." He started toward the door.

I grabbed the back of his shirt. "Not that way." I flicked my head toward the window. "It's more fun if we're sneaky."

"There you are," he said, and turned toward me.

"What do you mean?"

With the way Max smiled, we wouldn't need the moon to light the way. "Your daredevil is back," he said.

"Woo, Waffle House. Dangerous."

"Hey, don't make fun of my daredevil." He pretended to reprimand me.

I threw up my hands. "I wouldn't dream of it when waffles and bacon are at stake."

Max dropped his FSU hat onto my head, stole a much longer kiss, and followed me out the window and into the night.

It was only Waffle House, but he was right. Part of me—a part I loved—reemerged as we crawled out that window.

Thank God for Waffle House and Max McCall.

CHAPTER TWENTY-TWO

Friday morning, the sun climbed high in the sky, and I didn't dare argue with its pleasant attitude. Better sun than rain for Pirates and Paintball.

I toweled off after a long shower, knowing I wouldn't get another one until late Sunday night. As I packed, I imagined Trent tapping on my window with his pirate sword and asking if I thought this was the year he'd win. This would be the first Pirates and Paintball without him.

I whispered at his memory. "Sorry, friend. This isn't the year."

My phone buzzed.

Max: **I might need some help with my pirate costume.**

Me: **Okay.**

Max: **You ready?**

Me: **I hope.**

Max: **See you soon.**

I took some extra time to assemble my pirate costume and waited for five p.m., when all four families would descend on the McCalls's house. Mom watched for the Adlers and Garrisons through the living room window and clicked off the living room light when they arrived.

Five on the dot.

"All right, Sadie baby. Get your game face on," she told me.

I traced the scar up from my mouth. "Do I look tough?"

"You take everything too literally."

"You take everything too seriously," I said, shouldering my bags.

"You have what you need?"

I nodded, but she went through the checklist anyway. "Paintball gun? Sleeping bag? Pillow? Toothbrush?"

"Mom, I'm not a kid."

She continued. "Book? Pirate costume? Cards? Big?"

I nodded yes to everything except Big and kept nodding as she listed the contents of my entire bag.

"Hey, have you gotten any more of those envelopes in the mail?" she asked.

I said no, but I found it curious that she said Big's name and then jumped straight to the envelopes.

"Hmm. What a mystery."

"I told you. It's just a little joke someone's playing on me. Tell Dad to come on."

"As long as you're laughing. It certainly didn't start out that way," she reminded me. "Tony"—her voice echoed through our house—"come on. It's time."

Now, if I'd called my dad like that, she would have corrected me for yelling. I mentioned that and she popped me with a towel.

"About this weekend," she began. She held out two fingers and made the *I'm watching you* sign.

For sport, I made the motion back and held up my paintball gun. "I'm armed. Don't mess with me."

"No paintball in the house."

Like I'd shoot her right here in the living room.

Dad arrived, shouldered my bags, and said, "Is that some spunk I just heard?"

I pointed the gun at him.

He popped the top of my hat. "I like it, kiddo. Keep it coming."

They exchanged one of those looks I wasn't supposed to see.

"Wreck didn't make me blind, guys," I reminded them as we walked out the door.

They didn't respond, which was probably good for me.

Outside, at the dock, I witnessed the reunion of Gray Garrison and Max McCall. Made even more complicated by my appearance.

Here goes. I walked over to Max.

Max offered me his hand, offered me the choice to show

my allegiance. I put my hand in his.

Gray's jaw worked double-time, and he took a deliberate step away from the group. He knew, but it was still hard to watch. As Gray stepped back, Max stepped forward, keeping a firm grip on me—it was as if they were dancing—and stuck out his hand. "Gray." His voice gave an unfortunate squeak.

Gray accepted the handshake. "Max."

They both leaned slightly forward in a quasi-hug.

Max never had any trouble with Gray until Gray hurt me. Gray had been someone he looked up to and respected. Likewise, Gray had thought of Max as a little brother. But a little brother wasn't supposed to move in on his ex.

Greetings over, Gray and Max made themselves useful at the parents' requests. Gina and I drifted together. I waited for her to launch into an apology, but she kept her shit together better than I expected. We talked mundane things—Netflix shows, my new haircut, how long the eighties clothes trend would last—while all the things went onto the boat. When Dad asked me to pass him my bag, Gina's face became curious.

"Did you bring Big?" she asked. "I've missed that little guy."

Interesting.

Gray dropped the cooler he was lifting. "You brought the ugly blue beast?"

Interesting.

"He's never missed Pirates and Paintball, but alas, this year, I left him at home," I said to both of them, watching carefully for a reaction.

"Too bad. If you ask me, that bird needs a good paint job," Gray said. "I mean, Jesus, he's ugly."

"No one asked you," Gina said. "I, for one, am glad she left him at home, if you had plans to abuse him."

Interesting.

"Max"—Gray hefted the cooler onto the boat—"little piece of advice. If Sadie ever asks you to win her a stuffed animal, take off running and don't look back."

Gray wore a look of dissatisfaction as we boarded the boat, and I guessed why. For all his teasing about Big, the bird represented our history, and I wasn't carrying him around anymore. That obviously meant something different to Gray than it meant to me.

He went so far as to whisper to me, "You could have brought him."

"Nope, I couldn't."

There was no group hug this year. No champagne. No feting of Pirates and Paintball weekend. Mr. McCall simply reversed the boat and said, "And we're off." The engine chugged heartily beneath us, and the bay winked at us like an old friend. The bay waters were darker than the Gulf, not deeper in their entirety, but deeper close to the shore. The bay sometimes made me claustrophobic. It masqueraded as ocean, but was like a cheap imitation of the real thing.

The parents stayed in their place, up top, with one of the coolers. They'd promised to grill burgers and dogs in an hour. No surprise there. The menu was practically written in permanent ink in the galley. Tomorrow was waffles, sandwiches, and steak for dinner. They'd pretended they wouldn't make the usual homemade peach ice cream because it was too much trouble, but they'd make it. Routine was something they craved. I guess we did too, because the four of us plopped down in the stern and took our seats.

I checked my watch. We were five minutes away from Gray suggesting we play cards. Nertz, his favorite.

Gina took us on a short detour first.

"You still stuff Big with secrets?" she asked.

"Not secrets," I corrected her. "You guys always got hung up on that. I just put my thoughts in there."

Gray tugged his shirt to his lips and sucked on the top button. "Enough to drive you crazy, isn't it?" he said, flicking Max's chest. "There's no telling what she's said and thought about all of us."

"Hey, most of it's good," I argued.

"Most?" Gray repeated. "*Most* will kill a man. The gap between *all* and *most* is a canyon of suck."

"In my defense, we haven't had the best year."

Gina and Gray didn't comment. Max stretched a yawn into an arm around my shoulders.

"'Bout damn time we change that, if you ask me," Gina said after a minute.

Gray kicked his feet up on the seat and said, "Agreed. I say we play some cards."

Five minutes exactly.

No one argued. We fished decks from our bags and shuffled cards like pros. Minus the wind factor, Nertz was simple enough. At its core, it was a game of group solitaire, except with a speed component. Each player had to empty his or her hand, playing on the aces in the middle. The thing about Nertz was we didn't talk much, and if we did, it was rated R.

Some kinds of games lent themselves to filthy mouths. Cards was one of them. I always cussed at cards. Always. And I didn't feel guilty about it, because it was cards. That's how the game worked. Except none of us was allowed to cuss in front of the parents, and they were definitely within earshot.

Max had a clear advantage with those lousy vocal cords.

"Shit, McCall, you should let it fly. They'll never hear you," Gray said.

As soon as Gray said it, one of the parents yelled out, "Language."

Gray bridged his cards. They slapped onto the deck in that musical way cards do. "See," he said.

I seriously doubted we'd get in real trouble, but keeping it quiet was half the fun.

"I think they'd let us get away with anything tonight," Gina said.

"I even show up at something right now, I get a pass," I said.

"Lucky," Gray said.

"Right," Gina chimed in.

Gray's mom could be harsh, but we were all scared of Sonia.

Sonia could light a fire under any of us with wet matches.

"Since we survived the Cannon Balls incident, I think we can probably get by with a little language," Max said.

"Ohhhhh, the Cannon Balls incident. I'd almost forgotten about that," Gray said with an infectious laugh.

"Not me," Gina said.

"Me either," Max said.

Rock-paper-scissors, who's been sending me envelopes?

Unfortunately Gina called, "Go," and the Nertz game began before I could scavenge for any more information.

For the next hour, I didn't do anything except cuss and move cards from one pile to another. Unsuccessfully, of course. The cards, not the cussing. I was adept at that, a real natural.

Gray won—as he had most games of every year—which made him totally insufferable. He was a beast when it came to competitive things. With Max in the picture, insufferable meant unbearable. I used to think he was cute when he became so determined, working the top button of his shirt and demanding cards as if we were playing Go Fish.

As Gray sat across the boat deck from me, tossing cards on piles and claiming them, I remembered other Pirates and Paintball weekends and how, during all of those, we were together. Even with that thick neck, he was a sweet riot, and awfully cute with that crooked ear.

Not as cute as Max, but I saw Gray's good side again.

The elusive number three on the list—*Forgive Gina and*

Gray. And tell them the truth—could happen this weekend.

Would happen, I determined. Well, at least the second part. Forgiveness itself was like training for an Ironman: so many moving parts.

I still had a stack of cards when Gray screamed, "Nertz!" ending the game.

Gina dropped the f-bomb.

"Language!" three of the parents yelled.

"Sorry," she peeped like a bird.

Max nudged me. "You still with us?"

"I'm hungry," I said.

"Food break?" Max suggested to the group.

Everyone agreed. We left our cards on the deck and stormed the galley. Lucky for us, Mom was the keeper of all things carb. She piled Cheetos, chips, potato salad, and burgers onto fancy Chinet and sent everyone outside but me.

When they were safely on the other side of the door, she asked the question I expected. "You doing okay?"

"I am."

She pushed a little further. "Cross your heart?"

I swiped an X over my chest.

It wasn't a lie; I felt pretty good. But it made me wonder about the truths I'd kept to myself. If my life had been in the blender at the very moment Mom asked me, I would have given her the same answer. Was that wrong?

I imagined a world where my mother believed I was

undeniably happy. She'd had that for sixteen, almost seventeen years. That was a long time.

"You seem better," she said.

"Getting there."

"Are you comfortable with Gray? Gina? Is it weird that you and Max . . . I mean, with Gray here?"

"Yes. No. It's weird," I answered, and repeated what I'd started with: "I'm okay."

Mom and I hadn't talked about Max and me seeing each other since that day in the bathroom when she'd fixed my hair, but she was smart enough to know I wasn't going over to his house for mac and cheese.

I knew her opinion, though. Because I lived in a constant war with sleep, I'd overheard my parents' late-night discussions of Max and Sadie's love life. They were cautious, but pleased. Dad worried our ties with the accident could be dangerous or unhealthy. Mom said there was a reason for all of it.

I'd stopped listening after that.

"Where did your brain just go?" Mom asked, frowning. "You zoned out."

I took a sip of Mountain Dew, the syrup thick and sugary, and gave her another honest answer. "You don't want to know."

"Oh, go eat." She popped me on the butt. "Play cards."

I loved my mom so much in that moment that I almost dropped my plate and threw my arms around her. We were the kind of family who said I love you, so I said it then. Just so she'd know.

"You're the best," she told me. "And stop cussing at cards."

"Mom, *you* cuss at cards."

"Do as I say, not as I do, or whatever bullshit saying that is."

As usual, Mom was a clown factory.

I laughed all the way up the steps and onto the deck.

CHAPTER TWENTY-THREE

We docked the McCalls's boat next to their moored Jet Skis at a beach campground a few miles away from the little island.

"Who thought camping in June was a good idea?" Gray asked for the third time as the teenage contingent carted stuff off the dock and set up camp in the dark.

The heat index was in the high nineties and it was almost ten o'clock. We couldn't catch a breeze with a mitt. Unfolding the tent and lying on the nylon didn't help matters either. Everything felt sticky and gross. As Gray threaded poles through loops, he gave us instructions we didn't need. "No, stake it out tighter. Max, use the mallet. Gina, refold the tentfly or it'll get damp and mildew. Damn, it's hot." He went on and on, maintained that popping a tent was an art. We maintained that so was complaining, and he was king.

Beside me, Gina exhaled. "It really is hot, but I don't want to encourage him. He'll never shut up."

Gray Garrison could suck a bone down to the marrow.

He was still going. "Goodness gracious, Sadie May, take off the sleeve before I burn to death."

"Please don't call me that," I said. Trent was the only one of our group who had, and Gray knew it bugged me.

"You might want to change your email address if you hate it so much, but as you wish . . . *Sadie*." He overemphasized my name and kept going. "This wretched heat's making me ornery."

He sounded like Trent. *Wretched* was a Trent word. Max dusted the sand off his hands and muttered to me, "Not sure it's the heat," as Gina said, "Gray, we live in *Florida*. Where it's always *hot*. You might wanna move."

"Now who's being ornery?" He nudged me as if I might take his side. "Am I right, Sadie May? Or am I right?"

"*Gray*." I held an angry face for a full second. He was annoying as hell, but somehow he made us all forget about Trent's absence without letting us forget about Trent. I loved him for that. Laughter bubbled up from a place in my gut and infected everyone, which only added fuel to his fire.

When he'd gone on for another minute or two, Sonia, our temporary supervisor, added to the commentary. "Garrison, good Lord, put a sock in it."

Gray reminded Sonia politely that the parents slept on the boat. In the air-conditioning. With running water. And all the food. He invited her to trade places.

She invited him to go jump in the bay.

Which he did, drawing another chorus of laughter from everyone.

Trent would have been right on his heels, sopping wet and splashing his mom. Max, in a rare moment of solidarity, ran after Gray. Gina and I followed. Where one goes . . . the others follow. We splashed and dunked one another until we were properly happy and cool. I imagined the bay was our fountain of youth.

"You know what we should do?" Gray said.

"What?" we all asked.

Gray's answer was a terrible idea.

"Chicken-fight."

"In the dark?" Gina asked.

Gray skimmed his hand over a wave lit by the night sky. "By starlight."

I'd only chicken-fought with Gray against Gina and Trent, so I knew, once upon a time, I could take her every day of the week and twice on Sunday.

"You up for it, partner?" I asked Max.

"Hell yeah," he answered.

"Language," Sonia said.

Gray swatted Max's chest. "She got ya that time." He squatted down and gave Gina a boost onto his thick shoulders.

Max followed his example and I climbed on, hooking my knees beneath his armpits. If I had any doubts we were a couple

before, they ended with chicken-fighting. Gina and Gray ver-
sus Max and Sadie. This was our version of Facebook official.

"Bases aren't fighting," I called.

"That's no fun," Gray said. "I could take Squeak down—"

"Squeak?" Max lunged forward and locked arms with
Gray. We rocked backward as Gray broke the hold and shoved
him squarely in the chest. Max recovered; his feet found secure
footing, and his knees bent into an athletic stance. Props to
him. I wasn't heavy, but I wasn't a feather duster, either.

Gina and I had no choice but to engage. Old pros with new
partners. We scrambled at each other. Fingers intertwined, we
twisted and pinched and rocked to dislodge each other. Despite
the physical therapy, my arms weren't as strong as they used to
be. She was formidable, but also concerned she would hurt me.

"I'm fine," I told her when she went easy on me.

"Okay," she said, and tried a new move.

Below us, the battle intensified.

Gray and Max shoved and parried positions. Max was
stronger than Gray had anticipated. Long, wiry muscles broke
Gray's holds before he did any damage to our balance. The
game ended when Max dove at Gray and all four of us went
under together.

"Tie," Sonia yelled from the beach.

"No way," Gray argued. "We were up the longest."

"By half a second," I said.

"Exactly," Gray agreed.

Worn-out but no longer hot, we made our way to the tents

and forced ourselves to be productive.

Max whispered to me at one point, "Not bad for my first attempt."

"You've never chicken-fought before?"

"Odd man out," he said.

As soon as Max said it, I had a memory of him sitting on a cooler, his hands on his knees, watching. Now he'd made himself a participant. Ironically, while no one was watching.

Campground quiet hours were totally pointless, as we were the only people stupid enough to camp when it was this hot. Sonia made sure the tents were up and the genders separated, before she went back to her air-conditioned palace.

We all changed clothes, and since it was dark, I put on a T-shirt and shorts.

Max stole a private moment between the bathhouse and the tents. "I've had fun today," he said, and kissed me.

"Me too."

I buried my nose in his fresh shirt and took a drag of Max: bar soap, aloe, and sea salt.

"Sleep in it if you want," he offered.

On a scale of one to ten, having your boyfriend offer you his shirt scored 101.

I thanked him appropriately.

"Do I get to keep yours?" he teased.

I shoved him away and, despite the heat, slid his shirt over my own. "I'm heading out for a walk."

"Want some company?" he asked.

"Love some, but I need to unwind."

"You saying I wind you up?"

I bit my lip and grinned. "Maybe."

As I got away from him, his voice crept up as high as it could go. "Go write something sweet about me, and put it in Big."

I'd already done it. Just before I'd walked to the bathhouse, I'd torn the corner of a weathered band poster from a wooden pole and written:

Max McCall keeps surprising me with his strength.

I'd stuff it in when I got home. I imagined a parallel universe where there was another version of me. That me had a Big, some excellent resolve, and wrote things like that about herself: *Today, I surprised myself with my own strength.*

As I walked farther from the campsite, I rehashed my list. In the past week, I'd driven a car. Not on the road. Not even forward, technically, but I'd sat in Metal Pete's yard and shifted an old Civic from park to drive and back to park. Tonight, I'd chicken-fought and played Nertz with Max, Gina, and Gray.

Progress.

Maybe forgiving Gina and Gray wasn't letting go of what they'd done or dulling it down. Maybe forgiveness was giving the past less power to hurt me. Or even building new memories that were stronger than the painful ones. We'd done a little bit of that tonight.

"What do you think, Trent?" I asked the breeze.

I conjured a picture of him. Earth-toned board shorts, a

light-blue Billabong tank top, and a pink trucker cap that hid his bleached-blond hair. The same clothes he'd worn on the day he died. I imagined what he'd tell me. The mental chorus of words came as they often did.

Hold on. Hold on. Hold on.

"To the grudge? Or to Gina and Gray?" I asked, frustrated.

Hold on. Hold on. Hold on.

CHAPTER TWENTY-FOUR

Early Saturday morning, Max scratched on my tent. Gina pulled a pillow over her face and groaned as I unzipped the tent. The sun stretched and yawned with me.

Max looked as if he'd been up for hours. He held up a Diet Coke and a Sharpie. I sipped on the Coke and rubbed my eyes before I realized I was still in my shorts in the daylight. Tennessee and Pink Floyd said hi to both of us.

"I'm trying to stop," I said to Max, putting the Sharpie back in his hand. We'd discussed my Sharpie problem at length one night by instant messenger.

"No. No." He tapped his bare chest. "I need a treasure map."

"You want me to draw on you? What time is it?"

"*Too* early," Gina moaned from inside the tent.

"It's pirate time," Max answered as loudly as he could. He kicked the bottom of the tent. "Up and at 'em, Adler."

She groaned again.

I unzipped the tent halfway. "Let me put on some pants, and I'll draw your treasure map."

He stopped the zipper and tapped his throat. "Does my voice bother you?"

"You know it doesn't."

I never even thought about his voice unless I had to have him repeat something. I let him zip the tent to the top and took the Sharpie.

Max of small victories struck again.

I penned a pirate map worthy of Blackbeard. Drawing on myself was therapy. Drawing on him was sexy. The dotted line led this way and that, but ended at his heart. I circled a big X and handed him the Sharpie.

Tucking his chin, he admired my work. "Nicely done."

"Expert," I said with a shrug.

"You'll have a pretty sweet costume yourself."

I'd showed it to him yesterday, and he'd approved. In preparation, I'd cut a pair of black sweatpants off below the knees and doctored a Goonies sweatshirt so Tennessee wouldn't show. A dark do-rag covered Idaho, and two skull-and-crossbones tattoos were the finishing touch. Mom and I tested them out at home last week. The scar at my mouth nearly disappeared beneath the tattoo film. Too bad I couldn't wear these every day.

All this . . . and I got a paintball mask. Game, set, match. I should be on top of the world, but I wrung my hands instead.

Crowds still made me nauseous.

"Stick with me," Max said.

The problem with that suggestion was we didn't have control over registration. "We'll probably end up on different teams."

"If we do, odds are you'll end up with Gina or Gray," he said. "They both know this is hard for you."

Fear was such a thief. I loved the wildness of the game, the quickness of my heartbeat as I stalked across the island, the celebration of nailing a competitor. There was a barbaric nature to it—like living in *The Hunger Games* and knowing you're a badass. And it was still hard to be here.

"What can I do?" Max asked.

I shoved into him and watched the smile I loved ripple across his face. "You're doing it."

"I used to avoid people. Remember?" he said.

I nodded. Neither of us cheapened our emotions by comparing them side by side. Neither was *worse* than the other. I might be too stupid to change quickly, but I wasn't too stupid to understand.

"Sucks, eh?" I said.

"Yep," he agreed.

Our eyes drifted out to the bay. We watched small waves slush from side to side, rocking against the shore like a fast metronome. March winds in June would make for a challenge during the game and a fun ride on the Jet Ski later. The Gulf could be a bitch on wheels. Maybe after Pirates and Paintball, we'd ride out of the bay and toward the horizon.

After mentioning the possibility to Max, he gave me a half-cocked grin. The grin of someone who knew something I didn't know. "Sounds perfect," he said.

"What are you hiding, Max McCall?"

He toed the ground, shoved his hands into his pockets, and put on a pleased-as-punch grin. "I'll tell you after the game."

"Bad?" I asked automatically.

"It'll push you a little. Like a tank top or Pirates and Paintball. But not bad."

Worry dug a ditch in my chest. That sounded like a *From a friend who cares* statement.

Rather than spend the whole day wondering, I found a question to ask that wouldn't give anything away. "This doesn't have anything to do with Big, does it?"

"Nope, why?" he said quickly.

Maybe too quickly.

"No reason."

"I didn't mean to get you all worked up. You want me to just tell you now?" he asked.

"No." If it wasn't about Big, I wanted something to antici-pate. And if it *was* about Big, I wanted to keep the fantasy of us a little longer. "Keep your secret, Max McCall."

"I plan to," he said with a wink.

For the rest of the morning, he gave away nothing but a few dozen smiles.

CHAPTER TWENTY-FIVE

Some Emails to Max in El Salvador

From: sadiemaykingston@gmail.com

To: tothemax@thecenter.es

Date: March 14

Subject: my list

What do I want?

I want . . . so many things.

I'd like to drive a car again.

I'd like to live one day without thinking about my scars.

I'd like to walk the graduation line.

Maybe kiss someone without flinching.

See the Fountain of Youth.

Fletcher had me make an actual list. He asked me to pick

a number. I picked seven, because I always pick seven. Then, he told me to write down seven things I wanted. Seven things I thought were impossible. It wasn't hard. I could have listed a dozen, maybe more.

The funny thing is . . . if I'd made a list before the wreck, none of these things would have been on there. In fact, my list would have had things like:

Learn Spanish.

Go skydiving.

Visit the Great Wall of China.

I had all these pie-in-the-sky dreams, and now I have reality. I guess that's life for you.

What would be on your list?

Love,

Sadie

From: sadiemaykingston@gmail.com
To: tothemax@thecenter.cs
Date: March 20
Subject: your list

Max,

That's a good list.

Here are my thoughts:

1. If you ever do get that tattoo, I want to go with you.

2. I've done that. Two tips: make sure you enter the water completely straight, and follow the bubbles to the top.

3. Ha, ha.

4. I think LOTR was filmed in New Zealand. That's the closest Shire there is.

5.–6. Star Time can be anywhere.

7. Gross. You're such a boy sometimes.

Love,
Sadie

P.S. I saw Gray sitting on the curb across the street from my house this morning. That sounds creepy, but it wasn't. It looked like he was crying, which made me tear up too. Seeing him so vulnerable made me realize I don't have feelings for him anymore. And I think that has more to do with you than it does to do with him.

From: sadiemaykingston@gmail.com
To: tothemax@thecenter.es
Date: March 28
Subject: No hiding

Max,
I haven't been trying to make you read between the lines. You know I have feelings for you.

Love,
Sadie

From: sadiemaykingston@gmail.com

To: tothemax@thecenter.es

Date: April 2

Subject: ☺

Max,

You make me happy too.

Love,

Sadie

CHAPTER TWENTY-SIX

Max busied himself with Jet Ski maintenance.

I busied myself watching him.

The machines were cradled in two floating slips. In a few hours, the four of us would ride to the little island and register for the game. The parents didn't play anymore. Mom had taken exactly one paintball hit four years ago and declared she was no longer in her paintball years. The dads begrudgingly agreed to let the kids shoot paint; a concept they came to appreciate, as it allowed for beer and adult conversation. When the air horn blew, they'd idle out to the bay, drop anchor, and listen to the game from a distance.

It was just as well. I'd been the one who fired that ill-taken shot on Tara Kingston. I never 'fessed up to that one either.

Max checked the gas and opened the compartments under

the seat while I folded the tarp, cleaned off life jackets, and knocked away cobwebs.

These Jet Skis were old friends. I'd loved zooming over uncountable waves with Gray riding behind me, the wind whistling in our ears, wrapping around us like a blanket. Hell, the four of us lost whole days tooling around the bay, exploring, telling our parents we were going only a few miles, then ending up halfway to Panama City. Trent and I were the ones who pushed the other two out into the Gulf; there were too many no-wake zones in the bay. The ocean was a backyard for our inner daredevils, and we let them play.

Max zipped our paintball guns into his backpack and when he looked up, said, "You're smiling."

"I like to Jet Ski," I said, as if I were discovering it for the first time.

He looked as if he were discovering me for the first time.

"I remember."

We spent the rest of the morning on necessary tasks, like brushing our teeth and eating waffles. At eight forty-five, fifteen minutes before we were scheduled to leave, I found another envelope on top of my bag. In my tent.

Gina and I won Pirates and Paintball today. We sort of cheated.

That note was from three years ago.

Damn. Whoever did this, if it wasn't Gina, took a huge risk

of being caught. I peeked my head through the zipper and surveyed the group. Everyone was chatting it up by the shore. No one appeared to be the least bit curious that I was in our tent.

If they were going to play it cool, so would I.

"You coming?" Gina yelled.

"On my way."

I placed the envelope in the bottom of my bag, re-zipped the tent, and ran toward my friends.

The sun boiled us as we prepped the Jet Skis. We didn't discuss riding arrangements, and that was a relief. Gina crawled on behind Gray, and Max held up the keys as an offer.

"I'll drive," I said.

Dust flew off my words.

We slid the Ski off the slip, climbed on, and Max settled his hands on my hips, his thighs next to mine. Before I turned the key, I put my hands on his knee. He leaned in close enough to make me shiver.

"You thinking about winning?" he asked. His hands inched up my back and his breath touched my ear.

Damn. "Not anymore."

"Drive, Kingston," he instructed.

I took a deep breath as the engine roared and vibrated beneath us.

"Y'all have fun," Sonia called.

"Take care," my mom added. She used her patented Mom look to give me something extra.

"We will," I promised.

The rest of the parents waved and wished us luck.

The little island was only a few minutes' ride. It was the perfect location for Pirates and Paintball, and I had to admit to myself, I felt a little trigger-happy.

The sun played peek-a-boo with a cloud, but the winds felt as if they were straight out of Kansas. I handled the Jet Ski like an expert, and Max squeezed his legs against mine and tightened his arms around my waist. *Good job, winds.* I leaned into his chest until our life jackets touched. Windblown hair, oversize sunglasses, and a handsome pirate boy next to me: crowds be damned, today was fantastic.

That's what I told myself, and for once, I listened.

The closer we drove to the island, the more traffic we saw. Pirates and Paintball had a large following this year, larger than any of the previous years. There must have been over a hundred people on the shore gearing up and registering.

We ran the Ski up on the sand and crawled off the seat, stretching. Last summer, we'd ridden from fill-up to fill-up without getting sore, but this was my first ride of the season. And Max's, too.

"Look at all this," Max said.

There was plenty to see. Everyone waved and yelled out pirate-y things like "Matey" and "Har, har" as they passed us. No one said jack shit about my face. I saw one guy who could be Johnny Depp's brother, but mostly people paired eye patches, plastic swords, and gaudy necklaces with their guns.

We unzipped our life jackets in unison. Max's chest was

tanned and taut and only slightly smudged from the salt spray. The ropy muscles he attributed to building houses and climbing were lovely.

For an instant, I wished I had on a swimsuit. If only I could show off my hard-earned running muscles without revealing Pink Floyd and Tennessee.

Max lifted our guns and locked his backpack in the storage compartment. "You ready to kick some ass?" he asked.

"Uh, yeah," I said, more confidently than I felt.

"You two are toast," Gray taunted.

"In your dreams, Garrison." I pulled my trigger finger a few times in his direction.

"Sadie is pretty much a beast," Gina agreed.

Gray poked Gina in the ribs. "You're supposed to be on my side."

"We don't know whose side I'm on yet, dude," she said, flipping her hair. "I just might have to take *you* down."

I looked at my old friends in this familiar place and realized I'd found another tiny piece of myself. The moment was so perfect, I chugged it like a Gatorade.

Max noticed and kissed me on the temple. No flinch from either of us. I was glad he did it in front of Gray, but it sucker punched the conversation.

"Come on, gang. Let's go register." Gina threw an arm around my shoulder like old times. She didn't realize she was touching Tennessee. I let it go without comment.

We all stepped out and followed the crowd.

No one lived on the little island, and I had no clue who owned it. There used to be No Trespassing signs, which everyone ignored, but they'd been gone for several summers. Maybe the city bought the property, because private groups had rented it for all sorts of things: concerts, events, fireworks, and games like Pirates and Paintball. The island was small enough that you could walk around its circumference in two hours; Gina and I had done that plenty of times when we docked here to picnic and swim.

"Thank you for giving me this weekend," Gina said.

"I'm happy I could."

Her head tilted into mine. "After this weekend, can we talk?"

"Talk-talk?"

She nodded. "I have a confession I need to get off my chest."

I succumbed. "Okay. One rule: no apologies."

"I'll try."

"Then I'll try too," I said.

Give me a frickin' medal. I'm actually growing as a human being, I thought. Forgiveness was going to be my bitch by the end of this thing.

The registration team clearly wasn't expecting this many participants, so we waited forty minutes to pay our twenty-five-dollar fee. The lady taking money, Marge, had been with Pirates and Paintball since it began. Max and I both recognized her immediately. There weren't many women who wore a striped pirate tube top quite like her. A talent indeed.

Her hands clamped over her mouth, and she crawled under the table, through the sand, and popped up beside us.

"You *came*." Her delight was plain to see, as well as her cleavage. I squirmed a little as she slapped a hug on me without warning. Max raised his eyebrows, and I swear, somewhere in the ether, Trent giggled.

"Wouldn't miss it. Right, Sadie?" Max teased me.

"Nope," I said, even though I'd come up with a million excuses to do just that.

Marge handed us two mesh jerseys, one green, one blue. "Green's for the privateers. Blue's the pirates. Take your pick, kiddos."

I gave Max the *See, I told you this would happen* look.

We chose and she wrote down our numbers under the respective team names.

"Thanks, Marge," he said.

Marge thumbed toward a large gathering of players standing around the starting point. "Just think, sweetie . . . All this energy . . . Your brother would have *loved* it." She patted us on the shoulder and shoved us on our way in one motion. "Next," she called, because the line really was out of control.

Behind us, Gray plopped down fifty dollars for both his and Gina's registration.

"They look . . . snug," Max noted as we drifted toward the makeshift store that Xtreme Paintball, another sponsor, had set up under a tent.

"Yep," I agreed, not letting my mind backtrack to other snug images.

Tommy, the vendor, waved us over. "Here're two of my favorite people. What can I do you for today?" he asked.

Tommy was the sort of fellow who could say something like that, and you believed him. He was retired Air Force, had biceps the size of my thighs, and a wicked little scar above his eye that he'd picked up on a classified mission. Or at least, that was the story he told. I loved Tommy fiercely for that scar. Even more now that I had my own.

Max thrust out his hand, and when Tommy shook it, Max nearly came off the ground.

"Hey, Tommy," I said, and leaned over the merch table to plant a kiss on his weathered cheek.

He pointed to my face and nodded his approval. "You've been adding some serious character, Sadie Kingston. I like it, kid. I like it. We need to trade war stories."

Three extraordinary things happened.

One, I didn't automatically recoil or feel attacked.

Two, I imagined I was a hero like Tommy. That I'd gotten Idaho and Nameless while escaping from an enemy camp.

Three, I stepped out of myself, lifted the do-rag, and showed him the narrow, pink trenches on my forehead.

"I call this one Idaho," I said.

CHAPTER TWENTY-SEVEN

"Damn, girl." Tommy clapped his hands in applause. "That's cool as grits. Maybe I'll name mine now."

Oh, why not go with it, I thought.

"You'll have to let me know if you do."

Tommy winked at Max. "Don't let her go, man. Any woman who can fire a gun and wear a scar as pretty as that one is a keeper."

Tommy's words were worth more than a hundred sessions with Fletcher, because I *heard* them.

"That's the plan, Tommy," Max told him.

"Thank you." I stuck those words deep in Tommy's heart.

"All truth," he said.

We got back to game preparation after that. Max needed

two bags of paintballs and some CO2 cartridges, but Tommy wouldn't take any payment.

"On the house today. Special-occasion scar bonding," he claimed as he helped Max fill our gun hoppers and extra ammunition clips.

Before we left, Tommy leaned over the merchandise and said to me, "I was worried you wouldn't come this year. Your dad said you'd had a hard time of it." He pointed to the scars again. "Don't let anybody give you any shit out there. If they do, send 'em to me."

"Thanks, Tommy."

"We're all pulling for you to win," he told me.

I was pulling for me too.

"Wish you'd listen to me the way you listened to him," Max said when we cleared the tent.

I traced the X I'd drawn on his chest that morning. "I listen to you."

Everywhere we walked, Max drew a crowd. Pirates and Paintball veterans slapped his shoulder and welcomed him. People doled out careful sympathy, not wanting to tip a festive occasion toward sadness, but also not wanting to ignore his loss. Candace Rew, Max's *friend* from sophomore year, also seemed happy to see him.

Candace examined me a little too long.

"Hey, Max. Hey, Sadie." Her voice sounded like plastic knives.

I didn't pay her many words more than *Hi*, but I paid her attention. Curvy and sexy. She had perfect hips, boobs that made me envious, great ponytail hair, and a face that hadn't been through the window of a Yaris.

She hugged Max longer than I deemed necessary. I seriously considered wandering back to Tommy, but when Max felt my gravity shift in that direction, he accosted my hand. Candace, lovely Candace, looked quite confused.

I wondered . . . if she'd written Max emails all year, would she be the one with him today?

"Which team did they give you?" I asked, since she wasn't wearing her jersey yet.

Candace rolled her eyes. "Pirates. I always want to be a privateer and every year, I get stuck with this ugly blue jersey. Privateers just sound more sophisticated than pirates."

I knew one blue-jerseyed pirate—me—who had zero plan to be sophisticated. I'd rather be on Candace's team than let her cozy up to Max somewhere on the island.

"Jealous?" Max asked as we walked away.

"Nope."

"Liar?" he asked again.

"Yep."

Maybe I understood Gray better right then than ever before. Jealousy was fast on the take.

"There's no need," he assured me. "Old news."

Candace wasn't the only roadblock we met. Everywhere

we walked, we overheard conversations.

"Damn. That kid looks like his brother."

"Who is his brother?"

"Trent McCall."

"Oh."

"The girl with Max . . . was she the one in the front seat?"

"Think so."

"Shitty hand to be dealt."

We tried to ignore them, but every comment was a barb that dug into our hearts. Especially the people who said, "Who's this Trent dude?"

Only the person who loved Pirates and Paintball more than any of you! I wanted to scream.

Moving away from the bulk of the crowd, we tested our weapons in the little area they'd set up. The weapons were sound, and much to my relief, I nailed the target. Feeling satisfied, I asked Max to toss me my jersey.

"It matches your eyes," he said as I slid it over my Goonies sweatshirt.

"I'd still rather be on green with you."

With everything done, we needed to rendezvous with Gina and Gray. When I spotted them near the water stations, I snuck up and mimicked Trent's animated voice from years past. "Pirates and Paintball!"

That made them both whip around with a smile.

"Nicely done," Gina said.

"One of us had to say it," I told her.

Gray raised one hand and placed the other over his heart. "I hereby declare the banner passes to Sadie Kingston."

"Hear, hear," Max chimed in.

"You guys know being nice doesn't mean I won't shoot your asses out there, right?" I teased them.

"Ladies and gentlemen . . . the warrior is back," Gray said.

I was back. And I wasn't the only one.

Trent had been the nucleus of our friend family. When we lost him, we lost our chemistry. Little by little, as we remembered the things we'd loved and shared with him, the genetic material began to reemerge. We were still a makeshift group without him, but a group. If we kept this up, going back to school would be easier.

If we kept this up, life would be easier.

The announcer blew the air horn and called, "Five minutes until Pirates and Paintball. Please listen up for a reading of the rules."

We tuned them out, knowing the rules backward and forward. Pirates and Paintball differed from most paintball games. It was typical Capture the Flag style, but had a kill-shot rule that allowed everyone to play a little longer. A hit to the face or chest—a kill shot—put you down, but any other hit on the body required two shots before you were out.

Max screwed the new CO_2 cartridges onto our guns and dumped extra paint into his pockets. Gina and Gray did the same.

It wasn't until the official call to assemble into teams that Gray put on a blue jersey from his bag, and Gina put on a green. Gray cut challenging eyes at Max, slung an arm around me, and asked, "Ready, teammate?"

CHAPTER TWENTY-EIGHT

Max swore, but it was more like a Nertz swear than a worry swear.

I mouthed, *This is going to be* so *fun,* and he blew me a kiss. Confident. Happy. Not jealous. In control of who he was and what he wanted. Ironically, he was all those things without looking like an imitation of his brother.

People weren't perfect, ever, but sometimes moments were. That one was flawless. It wormed its way into my history and onto a piece of mental paper.

Max McCall stepped into the sun and out of Trent's shadow.

Don't shoot me, he mouthed back.

I held up my gun. *Don't get in my way,* I advised with a wink.

Max touched the X on his chest before he followed Gina and a sea of green jerseys off the beach to the preassigned

meeting place for privateers. Those two would last most of the
game. Gina was a brilliant shot, and Max was light and quick
on his feet.

Gray and I had an edge. We'd moved and hunted this island
together since the games began, getting better and better every
year. One year Gray sweet-talked Marge into a different jersey,
so we'd be together. Other than that, we'd been lucky enough
to land on the same team.

"Gina swapped me," he said.

"I figured."

"Can't break up a team like ours."

Uh, actually, you can. You did.

I kept that thought to myself.

Some self-appointed team captain circled up the group
and gave us the winning strategy. According to him, half of
us would hunt for the flag, half of us would guard the flag,
and . . . another four of us were supposed to hide and wait for
everyone else to shoot one another.

"Not much on math, is he?" Gray whispered.

"Half and half, and four. Yeah, that equals a whole. Noted."
Our team captain was no General Patton.

Gray ignored all instructions we'd be given. "Where do
you want to go, Sadie May?"

I gritted my teeth. "Seriously? I'm armed, dude."

"You won't shoot me. I'm on your team," Gray said confidently.

"Don't tempt me."

Gray nudged me with the business end of his gun and said, "Let's just get out of here before Half-Half-Four Guy sees us."

No one went in the direction we headed, but Patton yelled at us to hide. Guess we were half of the elusive four. I picked up my pace and forced Gray to match me. Mr. Muscles needed to up his cardio game; he was breathing hard and a step behind. The island was small, but for paintball, it was a huge playing field.

"When we're here, I always feel like we're in an episode of *Lost*," Gray said as he ducked through the sea grass without disturbing it.

"Me too."

We were a five-minute hard jog from the beach when the air horn signaled the beginning of the game.

"Are we really going to hide out?" he asked.

"For a bit," I suggested.

Hiding meant we'd have to be quiet while, hopefully, the bloodthirsty competitors took each other out. That approach had worked the year Gina and I won, and it was worth an attempt today. The competitor in me awakened like a sleeping dragon. I didn't want to play; I wanted to win. Even if that meant sharing the honor with Gray.

"No one will think we took this direction. Limited coverage," he said.

"Shh."

He nodded, and together we dug a foot-deep trench. We both lay down in the dunes, sand crabs and sharp shells be damned. Like this, only a kill shot to the face could take us out. Around us, but not close, we heard the game being played. The *thwack* of CO_2 gunfire echoed from the north and an occasional scream of "I'm out! I'm out! Stop shooting!" carried toward us on the wind.

"A long way off," he assessed.

"Someone else could still be close," I whispered back.

"Sadie, look at me."

His words were so delicate, they felt like a walk around a glass shop.

I looked at him and for the first time, he didn't look away. He even lifted his mask above his eyes, which were as gray as his name.

"I want to tell you something," he whispered.

You. Gina. Max. Jesus, did I have *Tell me something* on my forehead?

"Right now?" I asked.

"Right now." He spoke loud enough to draw enemy fire. "Before I lose my nerve."

Sweat glistened on his forehead. I stared at those tiny beads, and a barrage of paint flew over our heads. Gray rolled over on top of me to shield me.

His body on top of mine transported me back to the last time he hovered above me.

The Yaris smoked. I was on the ground. Pain.

On the island, Gray said into my ear, "Hold still."

He fired two rapid shots and a girl walked off the dunes

with pink and yellow paint on her chest.

There was blood in my mouth. There was blood, blood, blood everywhere.

On the island, his body pressed against mine. Pinched me between him and the ground. "I think she was alone," he said.

I tried to sit up and couldn't. Gray pressed his shirt against my face. Gray said, "Sadie, are you okay? Sweetie, are you okay? Oh God. Oh God, I'm so sorry."

"Don't be sorry. I'm okay," I told Gray. I wasn't okay.

Island Gray rolled off me and whispered, "Seems we're in the clear."

I bulldozed those memories to the side with a steady, internal voice. *I do not have a time machine.*

"What I was saying before," Gray continued. There was the sweat again, gathering on his skin. Not from the heat of the sun, but from the heat of what he had to say. "He makes you happy. Max, I mean, and—"

"Gray, stop."

"I kissed you the other night, and I shouldn't have . . . I wanna say I'm sorry. Anything that makes you smile, after this past year, I'm on board. Even if it's not me."

"You don't want it to be you. You made that pretty clear last fall," I said, keeping my eyes on my gun sites.

"Gina was a mistake," he said. "There's a reason it happened and you wouldn't—"

"Wouldn't what? Understand? Because trust me, I would

rather understand *how* you and Gina ended up kissing than be left to my own theories."

"Really?"

My answer came slowly. Eye to eye. Pain to pain.

"Yes."

"Okay," he said. "Here you go. Gina wasn't driving the day of the accident. I was."

Gray's words sliced into me. The sharp knife of truth.

Fumbling for a response, I said, "You . . . can't . . . drive a stick."

"I know." Gray rolled onto his stomach. Tears fell from his eyes to the sand. "That's why the Jeep stalled out."

"But—" I squeezed the trigger of my gun so tightly that several rounds fired off toward the tree line. "Why would you risk that?"

Gray buried his face in the crook of his elbow. "It's complicated."

"More complicated than both of you lying to me, to everyone, for a year?"

Was this what Gina meant to confess?

He caught the fear in my eyes, and lowered his head again without speaking. He still didn't think I could handle what he had to say.

Righteous indignation overtook me. I put my mouth against his ear and gritted out two sentences. "I am *not* an effing china doll. Now, tell me the truth."

"If you think about it," he said, "you already know the reason. Trent broke up with Gina *for you*."

"No, *he didn't*." That was the refrain of my life.

"You don't know what she said happened. You weren't in our car." He cringed as he said that statement. "It doesn't matter. What does matter is the truth, and that you finally know. I swear to God, I planned to tell you. We both did, but then, there just wasn't any good way to do it. It felt like if we told you, you'd blame yourself, and I didn't think you needed any more pain this year. But that's clearly *Not. A. Problem*. You don't even blame yourself for messing with our relationship and theirs."

I shook my head in disbelief. "What the hell are you talking about? I don't have to blame myself because *I didn't do anything*. I certainly didn't drive a vehicle that I don't know how to drive."

The fight drained out of him. He wore guilt like I wore scars. When he spoke this time, there was hardly anything left. "Sadie, you nearly died. I almost lost you. I could barely wrap my head around that. And losing Trent . . . knowing I killed him . . . can't you see how confusing this has been for me, too? I was angry with him, and you, and then me. It's been a damn carousel. So, hate me if you want, but I couldn't, wouldn't, pull another rug out from under you. And then, it was too late."

"I . . ." The words stopped. Nothing came.

Gray wasn't usually a crier. Now, his eyes and nose leaked in a constant stream. "What happened to you and Trent and Max . . . It's all my fault."

I stood up, vulnerable to the playing field.

Thwack. Thwack. Thwack.

Two shots pounded me in the arm. Another shot exploded against my leg. Purple paint splattered against my shin. I was out. But I wasn't playing the game anymore.

"Please say something," Gray said. "Anything."

"I don't know what to say. What am I supposed to do with this?" *Thwack. Thwack. Thwack.* I got nailed again on my hip.

"Blame me. Hate me. Punish me. Anything you need. I just want this . . ." He balled up his fists and pressed them into his thighs. "I want this . . . to be behind us."

I said nothing. I felt everything. I wanted to shoot him.

Gray read the cacophony of feelings perfectly. He stood up and faced me. "Shoot me, then."

Thwack. Thwack. Someone else took care of that for me.

"Sadie, shoot me."

"You're already out."

"You know you want to," he whispered.

I did—I wanted this anger to have a target—but I argued, "That's stupid, Gray."

"It's what I deserve."

"None of us deserved any of this."

Tears emptied out of him. "Please, Sadie."

I'd never been able to refuse a please from Gray Garrison. From six feet, I fired a single shot at his chest. One kill shot to the heart. I dropped the gun, unable to manage more than that.

He fell on his knees and cried.

Gray wanted to be punished, and I chose words instead of more paint. "I hate you for lying to me."

"I hated you for loving Trent."

"Trent was gay, you idiot."

Truth stood between us as still as a statue.

To me, that moment was like putting on contacts in the morning. The blurry world sharpened with crisp understanding. And regret. We'd lied. And lies, whether good or bad, always did irrevocable damage.

"You could have told me," he said. "It wouldn't have changed the way I loved him."

Gray Garrison: liar, heartbreaker, and beautiful friend to Trent McCall.

"No." I shook my head. "He should have told you."

"And now he can't."

"Now he can't," I repeated.

Gray's shoulders folded. He looked at Idaho and the scar at my mouth, forced himself to own his actions and misinterpretations.

This time, I was the one who looked away.

"I'm sorry . . . for everything," he said.

Even though I was sorry too, I didn't say it.

CHAPTER TWENTY-NINE

Some Emails to Max in El Salvador

From: sadiemaykingston@gmail.com

To: tothemax@thecenter.es

Date: May 10

Subject: nitty-gritty

Max,

Whoa, where did that come from?

I promise you that Trent and I didn't have anything going on. Ever. You are NOT stepping into his territory. You are not his replacement. You are also not a rebound from Gray. Please trust me. Oh, I wish I could explain how sure I am.

Love,

Sadie

From: sadiemaykingston@gmail.com

To: tothemax@thecenter.es

Date: May 12

Subject: RE: nitty-gritty

Max,

I can't tell you, but I am positive.

    Trent and I talked about it.

    I know that he didn't love me—except as a sister.

                        Sadie

From: sadiemaykingston@gmail.com

To: tothemax@thecenter.es

Date: May 14

Subject: RE: official?

Max,

Yes, I assumed we are a real couple. Exclusive.

    You don't?

                        Love,

                        Sadie

From: sadiemaykingston@gmail.com

To: tothemax@thecenter.es

Date: May 17

Subject: listen to "Better Together" by Jack Johnson

Max,

Just so you know, sometimes, when it takes you a while to
respond, it freaks me out. Especially after I send emails like the
last one.

I'm really glad we're on the same page. It's weird how
two people often worry about the same thing, and stew over
that thing, and create assumptions and fallout plans over that
thing . . . without ever talking about the thing. So let me say
this, loud and clear: I like you for you. Beginning and end of
story. I'm going to write that down and put it in Big right now.

Thank you for what you said about my face. I grant you the
freedom to change that opinion after you see me.

Okay, I'm going to hit send. Honesty is uncomfortable.

Love,

Sadie

CHAPTER THIRTY

I put my hands up in an act of surrender—for the game, for myself—and walked toward registration. My autopilot was set to the Jet Ski, and somewhere on the island, Max's autopilot was set to me.

Gray stayed on the ground.

Back on the main beach, paint splatters covered various pirate costumes, and participants who had lost sat on the sand recounting war stories, addressing blows to their pride with Miller Lite and suggestions of cheaters. I'd never been in this crowd before, and I had no plans to stay now.

My skin swelled in the few places I'd been hit. The whelps didn't compare to the hit I'd taken in the heart. Lies were like that. They barreled straight into deep tissue.

I made a beeline to the Jet Ski and sat down. Max appeared beside me wearing not a single fleck of paint. His hands on my shoulders, he gave me a quick hug, and looked me over, worried.

"I need to get out of here," I said.

Wordlessly, he gathered our stuff and waved away other curious participants who couldn't believe we weren't staying until the final horn. Behind me, Max apologized to someone—I didn't turn and look—saying we'd be back next year. I hated to leave Tommy and Marge without saying good-bye, but they wouldn't want to see me like this. I didn't want to see anyone.

Max stowed our gear in one of the Jet Ski compartments and swung his leg over in front of me, facing me.

"You want to talk?"

He was hoarse.

"I just want to go."

Max held out a life jacket. When I didn't react, he spoke to me the way I'd spoken to him at Trent's funeral.

"Forward is the only way through."

I wasn't trying to be difficult; my arms just wouldn't obey instructions. My brain was too busy being a washing machine, tumbling facts and histories over and over, drowning them.

They both lied to us.

I'd told Gray the truth about Trent.

I needed to tell Max.

Sliding the jacket around me, Max zipped it up as if I were

five. I felt his intense gaze and closed my eyes.

"We have to push off," he said, taking my hand.

Mechanically, we launched the Jet Ski into the water. Max drove without direction. His parents' boat lay anchored nearby, but he whizzed past them without acknowledgment. Max didn't flinch or answer as Sonia yelled to ask him where we were going. When we were no longer in sight of the little island or any of the boats, Max killed the engine.

"What do you need?" he asked.

"Open ocean."

"Done," he said, and we were driving again.

The world hazed around me.

I felt everything without feeling anything.

The puffy, happy clouds of the morning darkened like a bruise in the sky and threatened rain. Soon the threat was more than idle; we were dry one moment and under a waterfall the next. Rain plastered my bangs against Idaho and suctioned Max's clothes against his body. Nature, at its strongest, shaved off mountaintops or threw houses into the air, but it couldn't wash away pain.

Everything had limitations.

Max steered toward the curve of the horizon. I shivered from the wind and rain as we bumped along in the violent surf.

"It'll be warmer if we get in," he said, and slowed down.

When we stopped, I slid into the water, letting my life jacket keep my head above the surface. Max floated beside me, one hand on the Jet Ski, one hand on my back, as we bobbed up and down in the rain-pounded waves and searched the sky for lightning.

Max used the ocean and the rain to scrub the paint off my shoulder and arm and the tattoos from my cheeks. As if he knew I didn't want any evidence of today left on me.

"What happened?" he asked.

"Gray and Gina . . ."

He bent toward me so I wouldn't have to scream into the wind.

"They lied to us."

I told Max everything Gray had told me. I didn't know much else, and there were plenty of gaps in the story, but when I finished, Max gave a long whistle.

"There's something else," I said.

He swam closer to me.

"Something about Trent," I explained. "The thing I didn't tell you in my emails."

I'd told Gray without meaning to, but now, the words were stuck in my throat.

"O-kay," he said, preparing himself.

The rain hammered us. I took a deep breath, and lifted my own hammer of words. "You know that card in Trent's room? The one under his mattress?"

Max dropped his head in a slow yes.

"It was from Callahan."

Max looked up with questions in his eyes. He whittled those questions into a name. "Chris Callahan?"

"Yes."

"Are you saying what I think you're saying?"

"Yes."

"I . . . Does anyone else know?"

"They didn't. I just told Gray."

"You didn't tell me first." It was both a question and a statement.

"I didn't know how."

"All those emails where I was worried about—"

"Max, he hadn't told anyone yet, so it felt like a secret I was supposed to keep."

"He told you," he said accusingly. "And you told Gray instead of me, when I'm his brother."

"I didn't mean to. I told Gray in anger. I'm telling you now—"

Max finished the sentence for me. "Because you have to."

"Maybe," I admitted. "But I'm glad you know. Trent didn't want to tell you."

"Why?"

"He didn't want to change things."

"That asshole."

"Max, put yourself in his shoes. It's terrifying to live one way and then try another."

"I could have handled it. I could have helped. You should have told me."

But I hadn't. And nothing changed that.

Lowering his chin to the water, Max scooped up a handful

of ocean and let it drain through his fingers. Any other words he had followed the water to the bottom of the Gulf.

"What do we do now?" I asked.

He bent his neck, his head hanging there like fruit on an overladen tree. "Sadie"—my name sounded hollow—"let's go home."

The tides of us changed in an instant. We came out here for me. We were leaving for him. "You okay?"

Max delivered his thoughts swiftly and quietly. "I don't know what I am. They lied, and they have to live with it. You lied. Trent lied. I have to live with that. I need some time."

"But Max . . ." I stopped myself from arguing, from making things worse. He had every right to feel the way he did.

Without another word, Max climbed on the Jet Ski. Robotically, I followed. He forced me to the front, sandwiching me between his body and the steering column.

I zoned out while Max drove us to the dock at his house.

I went back to the day Trent told me about Callahan.

CHAPTER THIRTY-ONE

It was just another summer day where I was in love with my book and towel and sunblock. Trent snatched my paperback and said, "Don't live in that fantasy world; come play in mine."

"Does your world have motorcycles?" I said, reaching for the book.

He tugged me up from the towel. "I swear it does."

That phrase usually led to actual swearing, but that day he grinned ear to ear. I swore for both of us, and followed him off the beach. I complained about the heat of the sand. I protested that I was at the good part of my book. I asked where we were going.

Trent never gave something away unless he wanted to.

He marched me to the Yaris and drove us to the kiteboard shop where our friend Callahan worked.

"Callahan, toss me your keys," Trent said.

Callahan was a couple of years older. Sometimes we rented from him, but I didn't realize Trent knew him well enough to demand his keys. Callahan threw a wink and a key at Trent and said, "Bring it back with gas, bud."

"You were saying." Trent gloated as we walked to the Ninja.

The challenge bit me in the ass. He shoved a helmet on my head, and I hiked my leg over the seat and held on. Through town, Trent rolled slow. His balance was perfect and easy to match. Melding with him was like singing harmony; I went wherever he did.

"You're really good at this," I yelled.

If he heard, he acknowledged by increasing the speed. Trent rocketed us away from the coast and toward the part of Florida no one visits. Out where bales of cotton lay in the fields and abandoned peanut stands leaned between trees. Angling with him on the curves, leaving my hands on my thighs, I sat slightly to the right and watched our world streak by. The blur was beautiful.

My ponytail would be a rat's nest for days, but I didn't care. There were endless roads and endless smells. Pine. Leather. The lingering scent of coconut sunblock. The sun sat so high in the sky that it looked like the end of a flashlight.

And I was with Trent, the magician of unusual days.

When he opened the motorcycle up, my heart beat patty-cake, thrilled at the wind and speed. Somewhere between sixty and "Oh damn, that's fast," my hands locked around his stomach. I felt his laughter in my fingers as his belly shook with delight from scaring me.

A stop sign held us up. He dropped his feet to the ground and swiveled back to me. "Your turn."

I took my turn, and his instructions. Curves were hard to handle because of our weight ratios. The straight stretches were a different story. On the open road, I let the needle climb to 101 before I brought it back to reasonable and braked.

"Hot damn," Trent said. "Can't do that in a book."

I didn't tell him that I absolutely could, because he didn't understand fiction.

We swapped seats two more times, and got lost on the back roads until Trent pulled over in the grass and said, "Hey, I know this place. Take a walk with me, Sadie May."

I was game.

Game. (n.) my willingness to follow Trent McCall into the heart of Mordor, or the Forbidden Woods, or a field with a No Trespassing sign.

Long weeds kicked at his calves as he left the side of the road and took a few steps into a field.

"Come on," *he said in that breadcrumb way.*

"Right behind you."

Our shoes sank into the soft earth. As we arrived at the top of a tiny rise in the land, I saw more of what I'd already seen: a whole lot of northern Florida that was exactly like the rest of northern Florida.

Trent took off Callahan's jacket, spread it out, and gave it a pat.

Invitation accepted.

When we were on the ground, he angled toward me. "Sometimes the sky is my favorite photograph," he said.

"It's more like a movie," *I argued.*

"Not if you lock the perfect shots in." He tapped his temple and said, "Snap. Snap," as if he were taking a picture. "I'm keeping this one of you forever."

I shoved him over. "Please don't. I haven't brushed my hair in days."

"No one brushes hair in the summer," he maintained.

I agreed.

The sky was a denim-blue dome. A shade the ocean couldn't hit on its best day. I was as happy in this story as I'd been in the book.

"Dad used to bring me here when I was a kid," Trent said. "Usually there are jets."

"And Max?" I asked. "Did he bring him here too?"

"No, this was our spot. He took Max to the library." Trent's hands worked the field like a tiny plow, pulling up clumps of dirt and sand. "I've only been here with one other person."

"Gina?"

"Naw. We always go to her house." He shrugged. "She likes the couch."

"Who?" I asked. "Gray?"

Trent didn't answer. "You have anywhere in particular you go with Gray? You know . . . when the four of us aren't together?"

"Can't kiss and tell," I said.

"Not even with me?"

I debated my answer. Trent and Gray were tight enough to trade stories, but telling Trent was a slight betrayal of Gray. Not telling him, after he'd asked, felt worse.

"You know that salvage yard near Ferry Park? Metal Pete's. Well, sometimes we go out there and sneak under the back fence. There's this old RV and . . ."

I let Trent fill in the rest of the details.

"Nice," he said after a pause. "But not as nice as this field. I mean, look at that azalea. Metal Pete doesn't have those, does he?"

They were odd things to compare. Trent rolled his head toward me. His eyes were the same color as the sky.

He said, "Sometimes I wonder . . ."

"About?"

"Everything."

"Take one of your pictures and describe it to me," I said.

The skin around his closed eyes wrinkled like an old man's.

"Well, I think about graduation, and what I'll do with my life, and who I'll do it with, and if I believe in God, because I think I do. Nothing feels accidental. I think about how deliberate everything in the universe is when I see the ocean and know it's the moon that moves it around, or when I watch a crab digging a hole or a shark nosing through the water, or a jet leaving contrails, or even those azaleas over there. We're in the middle of nowhere, but they're beautiful. I want to be like that."

I tapped out a little rhythm against his thigh, letting the way he lingered on the word beautiful tickle my ears.

"You wish you were beautiful?" I asked, slightly teasing him.

He tapped his chest. "In here, Sadie May. I want beauty."

Trent was so serious, I nearly cried. "You have beauty."

My smile didn't inspire him.

"Doesn't seem that way. Life's more like that damn bird of yours. We stuff it full of moments we hope matter, but we can't tell until later if they do." He stopped and covered his face with his hands. "I wanted to watch the sky today, but now that we're out here and we're talking, I kind of want to tell you something."

"So tell me," I said. His knuckles were almost white with tension. I tugged his fingers apart until I could see one eye. "Hey, why are you so keyed up? It's just me, and we're lying here in a field on a perfect day. We rode a motorcycle so fast I practically pissed myself. I declare it to be a day of revealing secrets."

His face relaxed momentarily, but then the familiar wrinkles formed around his eyes.

"Here's a secret. I want to matter. I want to be known. I want to be myself. I want you to write this day on a piece of paper and put it inside Big. And one day, when you open him, you'll read about me and think, 'God, that day with Trent was one of my favorite days ever.'"

Caution crept into my voice. "Trent, what's going on? You sound worried about us."

"Just let me get this out, okay?" he pleaded. "I figured out it's possible to fall in love with two people at the same time. I figured out . . . it's very inconvenient."

My eyes wide open, I stared at my best friend. At his chin, and his forehead and cowlick, and long blond eyelashes: all the little details and pores and skin that made Trent who he was.

What was he saying? That he loved Gina? And me, too?

I loved Gray. No doubt. His was the only name I'd ever doodled on a folder. The only last name I've ever tried on as my own. Sadie Garrison. But . . . Trent was Trent, my Trent, and I loved him, too. I'd never asked what type of love it was, because it had always been so damn platonic.

I allowed myself to question it now.

I imagined a future where Trent opened the door to a coffee shop and bought me a vanilla latte with two shots of espresso, wondering whether it was in bad taste to ask Gray Garrison to be his best man at our wedding.

My imagination was so terrifying that I wanted to kill the thought before it took root. Tension filled Trent's face. This conversation was about to go to an uncomfortable place.

Trent pulled me toward him. "Sadie." He was so close, his breath landed on my lips, smelling like ChapStick and spearmint gum.

I was frozen in thought.

I thought about Gray. About ruining everything we'd built.

I thought about spearmint and how I love to taste it on my tongue.

I thought about that vanilla latte.

I thought about Gray again and how he hated coffee.

I thought about his sweet face and how it would leak hot tears if he found out I cheated on him with his best friend.

I thought about how this moment didn't have an exit strategy. How it was lose-lose. I would regret it if I kissed Trent, and I might regret it if I didn't.

"We can't," I whispered.

"Oh God," he said, face red, realizing my conclusion. "I didn't mean . . . I'm not saying I'm in love with you."

"Oh! I just thought from—"

"No, oh, no, I'm sorry. I'm really sorry." He laughed nervously. "It's not you. It's Chris."

"Chris who?"

Trent unpacked a smile I'd never seen before. "Callahan," he whispered.

Hot Chris Callahan who worked at the kiteboard shop. Sexy Chris Callahan with a five-o'clock shadow, leather pants, and the motorcycle we rode here on. Kind Chris Callahan who winked at Trent.

"Oh. Wow. Okay, then," I said. "Well, huh."

"Do you hate me?"

"Hate you? Of course not. Why would you even think that?" I said indignantly. We didn't have any gay friends, but I'd never given him any reason to think I'd judge him if he was in love with a guy instead of a girl.

"'Cause . . ."

He looked like a lost boy.

"Look, I don't care who you love as long as I get to be in your life," I told him.

He tucked a tangle of hair behind my ear and kissed my forehead. "Sadie May, you are a wonder of wonders."

"Well . . . you being in love with Chris Callahan is much easier than you being in love with me."

"What do you think about the others?" he asked.

The others were Gina, Gray, and Max.

"You need to tell Gina," I said.

He stared up at the sky. "Even if I don't have my head around this yet?"

"Does Chris know?" I asked pointedly.

Trent nodded shyly, and in a way that told me his feelings weren't one-sided.

"Then you've got to tell Gina something. She deserves to know," I said.

"You're right." He gave a slow, painful exhale. "But give me some time. I wasn't expecting to have these feelings, and I'm still not sure what I should do with them."

I pulled him away from the sky and back to my face with an honest question. "What do you want to do, Trent?"

"Understand."

That made sense to me. These weren't easy feelings to navigate.

"Okay," I said. "But if you follow through on those 'feelings'"—I threw some air quotes around the word—"and don't tell Gina, I'll kick your ass. Got it?"

He saluted. "Got it."

We lay there for a little while.

"You know Gina better than anyone. What will she say?" he asked.

I could only guess, but that didn't seem wise to do. "Trent, you can't know how she'll respond, but that doesn't mean hiding this is okay. Ya know, maybe she'll surprise you."

"Will Max and Gray hate me?" he asked.

"I don't think hate has a role in this. They'll be surprised."

"Were you?" he asked.

I raised my eyebrows. "Uh, remember that time I thought you were going to confess your undying love for me and then it turned out you were gay?"

He laughed. "I'm not gay."

I rolled my eyes toward him and latched my hand with his.

Trent tried out the words. "Okay, I might be gay."

That was far enough for one day.

"Thank you," he said.

"For what?"

"Understanding."

I wished Trent had given Max and Gray and Gina that same opportunity to understand.

CHAPTER THIRTY-TWO

Max stayed on the Jet Ski as I disembarked. His eyes were glazed over in thought and didn't meet mine when I asked, "Can we talk later?"

"I'm sure we can. I'll call."

That response was better than I expected.

I zombied my way inside, wondering if this was how Trent felt in that moment before he told me about Callahan—as if he might lose me.

Even though it was lunchtime, I took a long, hot shower, Sharpied my scars—even Idaho and Nameless—and crawled into bed feeling worse than I had in a year. How in the hell had life ended up like this? This was why we'd all lied. We wanted to avoid this explosion, and destruction came all the same.

I slept on that thought until late in the afternoon, when my parents returned early from Pirates and Paintball. Drawers and doors slammed shut as Mom and Dad put away camping and food supplies. I listened for their whispers among the noises, but they weren't talking. The crashing and banging sounds communicated enough. They were home . . . and angry.

Mom's footsteps echoed on the hardwood hall floor, slapping toward my bedroom door like Godzilla. My doorknob turned.

"Sadie."

Slam. She dropped my weekend bag on the floor and glared at me.

"What did you do?" she asked. Her voice pinched each word.

"I came home early."

"No. What did you do to your face?"

I slowly lifted the covers over my mouth and then over my whole head, remembering the Sharpie session I'd done before I'd fallen asleep. There was no explanation.

Mom walked over to the bed and sat down. "Baby, what's going on?"

I had a one-word answer. "Life."

"I thought you were getting better," she said, completely forlorn.

"I am better."

She tugged the covers down, peeled my hands away from my face, and held on. "Honey, this doesn't look better. This looks scary."

"I am scary."

She kissed me all over my face, like the Sharpie was a million boo-boos that needed her love. Over and over, with each kiss, she said, "Be okay," as if they were prayers.

Maybe they were.

When she finished, she didn't let go of my face. "Are you listening to me?"

She made sure I was.

"What you did today was rude and selfish. Leaving in the middle of the weekend. Not even telling us why. You left us to pick up your campground site and get your bag. You ignored my texts." She growled, and then sighed deeply. "Your father and I were . . . I don't know what we were, but this"—she squeezed my cheeks and softened her voice—"needs to be addressed first."

She stood up and left. When she returned, she had a package of alcohol wipes. Very carefully, in neat, gentle strokes, she cleaned the Sharpie off my face. I pushed up my sleeve for her to see Tennessee.

She cleaned it, too.

I lifted the covers, and let her see Pink Floyd.

There was so much sadness as she scrubbed away the damage I'd done to myself. In a quiet tone, as she threw away the supplies, she said, "I'm calling Dr. Glasson."

"Okay," I said.

"Where are your Sharpies?" she asked, as if they were drugs.

"In my drawer. The one beside my bed."

Mom slipped both markers into her pocket and walked toward the hall. When she closed my door behind her, she opened it again immediately. "I love you," she said fiercely.

Mom threw those sweet words at me, and I snatched them out of the air and tucked them to my chest.

"I love you too," I echoed back.

The door closed for good, and Mom retreated toward the kitchen. Toward the phone. Toward the safety net of my father and his jambalaya that boiled on the kitchen stove. He cooked when things were off. Sometimes at two in the afternoon; sometimes at two in the morning.

He cooked. Mom cleaned. I stared at the back of my eyelids.

But I didn't Sharpie any more scars.

Around me, the air-conditioning hummed and the ceiling fan rotated slowly, and the two little chains that hung down from the center globe clicked against each other—*click, silence, click*—and my fish swam in their gurgling prison. All familiar white-noise sounds that usually lulled me to sleep.

This afternoon they kept me awake and distracted.

Maybe an hour later, my bedroom door swung on its hinges and two fragrances crawled into bed without an invitation. Ocean salt and sandalwood, the scent of a million sleepovers.

Gina.

"I had to come," she said. "Please don't ask me to leave."

The duvet separated us. Her arm fell over me, and she wiggled as close as she could. Gina and I had talked for hours in this bed. About the guys, and nail polish, and sex, which clothes to wear, extra pounds from french fries, and . . . I could write a Tolkien-length book of things we'd discussed.

After a year of push-and-shove, I rolled over. Into her.

My best friend held me.

Anger or not, it was glorious.

"Gray told me what happened," she said. "I was going to tell you after this weekend."

I stayed tucked against her chest where I couldn't see her. She took a breath so deep, it was as though she used the air in my lungs.

"I'm sorry," she said.

If there was one thing I knew, it was that Gina Adler was sorry. But I hadn't known until today what she was sorry for. She worked her hands through the snarls in my hair as if she could somehow untangle everything.

"Why didn't you tell me the truth?" I asked.

Gina had an answer and question ready. "Because it wasn't just my lie. Or even one lie. Why didn't you tell me Trent was gay?"

"Same reason," I said.

Gina twisted a strand of hair around her finger until it was tight against her scalp, pulling so hard I was afraid she'd rip it out. I stopped her.

She and I had been friends since kindergarten. When you know someone that well, she reads like a newspaper. Smiles and frowns are front-page stories. Tears are obituaries and birth announcements. And little habits: they're the human-interest stories. This hair thing with Gina . . . she did that when she deeply regretted something.

"Can we tell each other everything now?" she asked.

"Please."

Gina thumbed down her eyebrows, massaging away the stress. She looked at my face, from the top of Idaho down to the scar at my mouth, and traced the lines with her index finger.

I let her. Max had kissed those lines and kept his eyes open. This was Gina's kiss. It was acceptance.

"I hate looking at you," she whispered.

"I'm aware."

"I hate it because I feel responsible," Gina said.

I focused on the fish tank instead of Gina's silent sobs. I wanted to put my arms around her, and eventually I did. She cried in earnest while the water bubbled in the tank and the fish swam in circles. I listened with my heart. And for once, I know she felt heard.

The memory of the wreck burned fresh in Gina's eyes when she spoke.

"Gray and I heard screeching tires and turned around. . . ." She cuffed the back of her neck and rubbed. "We watched it. Heard it. That sound of his car crashing into the tree—that's what I hear at night, and when I wake up, and when I look at you, and when I think about Trent."

"I hear it too."

She swept my bangs farther to the side and looked, really looked, at Idaho. "Gray probably said this, and you probably don't understand, but you were so hurt. And not just here." Slowly, she moved her hands from Idaho to Tennessee to the center of my chest. "You were broken here. We all were in different ways, and we just messed up."

She paused to breathe, but I continued to listen. To the silence. To her words.

"Gray and I thought we were saving you from more pain. But keeping that secret backfired. It created a weird . . . intimacy . . . a guilt pact. After you caught him kissing me, God, I knew all we'd done was make another scar for you to wear. And that scar had my name on it. Sadie, please understand, I couldn't bear to give you another scar."

I wiped her tears away, understanding the intimacy of secrets.

"You were hurting too," I said. "And you left me out of it. Hid it."

"We all did," she said.

"The real scar was that you and Gray chose each other instead of me," I told her.

"And you chose Max."

"Yeah, I guess so."

Gina pushed herself into a sitting position and lay against the headboard. I did the same. And when she placed her head on my shoulder, I leaned my cheek against her hair.

"Sadie?"

"Yeah?"

"Do you ever wonder what life would be like if we'd all just gone for ice cream together or didn't go to the beach at all, or if Trent hadn't chosen that moment to break up with me?"

"Every day."

We don't have a time machine.

"I don't know what would have happened, but I know what did," I said.

She knew too.

Once upon a time, there were four friends, two couples, who stopped being friends before they stopped being couples. Little questions niggled the back of their heads like splinters buried in the skin. Questions of trust and intention. Who loved whom the most? What if he wasn't the best person for her? What if she wasn't?

No one talked about the questions, because talking ruined plausible deniability. Talking burst the bubble of innocence.

Talking ended the happily ever after.

These were the truths they believed.

And they were lies.

They should have talked while there was still something to say.

"Look," I said. "I don't know what Gray told you, but you need to know, Trent loved you. That wasn't a lie."

She used my sheet to wipe her eyes. "It sure feels like it."

"You know Trent. He was an explorer," I said, trying to take what I knew about his feelings for Callahan and explain what he'd told me. "That's what he was doing. He was so uncertain of what he wanted, but certain that he loved you both. He was confused, and scared, and didn't want to confuse or scare you until he had his head wrapped around his feelings."

"You're positive?"

"You know I am. Love is just messy sometimes," I said with certainty.

Love, unlike relationships, wasn't simple math. Trent understood he couldn't be in a relationship with both Callahan and Gina, but he couldn't stomach changing the way he felt about either.

"How am I going to tell her, Sadie May?" he'd asked.

"I don't know."

He hadn't known either, but on June 29 last year, he'd taken the first step toward breaking her heart. In a terrible way, his last act had been incredibly brave.

"He wasn't trying to hurt you any more than you were

trying to hurt me," I said. Her head bobbed against mine in understanding.

Gina zipped her necklace charm back and forth, biting her lip. "Still hurts."

"Of course it does." I touched her hand, stopped it mid-arc. "But at least you can grieve the real thing now. Grieve it all the way to the end."

"So can you."

We both sank deeper into the pillows, exhausted by the efforts of verity.

"Can we find a way to be friends again?" she asked. "I don't want to do this without you anymore."

"I hope so. I don't want to do this without you, either."

Forgive Gina. *A posse ad esse.*

I had a question for her, but I needed to clear up one more thing first. "Have you been putting letters in my mailbox?" I asked.

"No."

It was a simple answer and I believed her. There was no reason to lie now, and she wasn't even curious. I leaned against her, relieved, and Gina opened her eyes.

"We're okay."

"On the road to it," I confirmed.

She exhaled and then kissed my cheek, just above Nameless. "I'm gonna go home and sleep for a week," she said, crawling out of my bed. "My soul is tired."

"G, would you do me a favor?"

Her face lightened considerably. "Anything," she said.

"I want to go to St. Augustine. To the Fountain of Youth. Will you go with me?"

"I'll go anywhere you want."

Now I was the one with bread crumbs.

She squeezed my hand, I promised to call, and she went home to rest her soul.

CHAPTER THIRTY-THREE

Max didn't respond to calls, texts, or emails.

The next morning, he wasn't in the hammock with a book and he didn't come to his window when I pecked on the glass.

I made a blanket fort in my bedroom, reread *Peter and the Starcatcher*, and prayed my phone would buzz. He'd said he'd call.

He didn't.

He'd felt closer when he was in El Salvador.

CHAPTER THIRTY-FOUR

There was still no word from Max the next day as Mom and I cleared away the breakfast dishes. I'd tried everything I could, short of banging on his door and demanding that Sonia tell me where he was. Silence was the price of keeping secrets.

Mine piled up like dirty laundry.

At Mom's insistence, our little family planted ourselves like spokes on a wheel around the kitchen table. This talk smelled of pancake syrup and Clorox.

I groaned as Mom slid another envelope across the table and into my hands.

"Open it," she instructed.

"Here?"

Her eyes nearly bugged out of her head.

I prayed as I tore the end of the envelope and took out the

paper. *Please don't be about sex. Please don't be about sex.* I had a feeling God wasn't listening to that request. Not that God is smug, but I pictured Him sitting back on a beautiful golden throne, steepling his fingers, and saying, "Sorry, Sister Sadie, you got yourself into this one."

Dad leaned toward me, prepared to read over my shoulder. "Stop stalling," Mom said.

Our kitchen was her courtroom.

I unfolded the letter and read aloud:

```
The five of us broke into the community center
tonight because Trent decided we needed a
dance-off. I came in dead last, Max won, and I
laughed until I cried. I'm really lucky to have
my friends.
```

There was no sweet *From a friend* closing. Since I'd narrowed the culprit to Gray or Max, that made sense. Neither of them was talking to me.

"What does that mean?" Dad asked. He checked with Mom instead of me.

Just then my parents seemed young and unsure. Maybe no one put this type of crap in the parenting magazines and books they scoured. Or maybe, thirty-eight equaled wise on most things, but not wise on all things.

I lifted my shoulders in a half shrug. "No idea, Dad. I've been getting these things since the beginning of June."

My shrug was worth a wooden nickel to my mother. "You know more than you're saying."

"Mom, I *don't* know." I wasn't about to accuse Gray or Max in front of them.

"You don't have a clue who wrote that?" Dad asked.

I bit my bottom lip and proceeded cautiously. "Well, yeah. They're my words, but I sure as heck didn't send this to myself."

"You wrote that?" Mom repeated the words as a question, even though she already knew the answer.

"It's one of the things I put in Big." I explained that every envelope contained something I'd previously written and stuffed in Big, and I had no idea how anyone had access, much less why they were sending me these things.

Also, that I wasn't worried.

Right. That last part was a whale of a lie, but after the weekend, I needed to de-escalate Mom and Dad's anxieties.

"I don't even know what to say," Mom said, eyeing the paper as if it were a snake.

"Me either," I said.

Dad examined the envelope and found exactly what I had. Nothing.

"You broke into the community center," he stated again, massaging his forehead.

I tempered my reply. "Well, sort of. Someone left the alley window wide open, and we crawled through. Just . . . you know, for fun. We didn't hurt anything."

"Sadie." Dad's voice came with a warning.

"Dad, Trent volunteered there all the time," I said, hoping to calm him down.

Mom was on the same wavelength. "Tony." She patted the air, a warning to both of us.

He chewed his thumbnail and searched for a response. Mom put her head on the table as if the whole thing were too much to handle. They were in a delicate catch-22. Battling me on the content of the note might push me into an emotional hole, which they didn't want to do. Not battling me meant I might engage in stupid behavior again, which they didn't want me to do.

"It was a long time ago," I said.

"And these other envelopes you've gotten, do they have other such . . . frivolity?" Dad asked.

"Tony," Mom said again.

Frivolity? I exhaled at his use of vocabulary, but his eyes sliced into me.

"Yes, Dad. I believe before Pirates and Paintball you referred to it as spunk."

"I'm all for spunk, but not so much for the *criminal behavior,*" he said.

It was Mom's turn to roll her eyes. "Tony, you're the one who used to steal street signs at her age."

I put my head down so I wouldn't laugh at Mom busting his chops. Dad stood up, wagged his finger at Mom, and said, "This one is all yours."

In the end, Mom folded the envelope, put it in her pocket,

and announced we were going to be late for therapy. "Talk to Dr. Glasson about all this," she said.

Family meeting over and done . . . with slightly more syrup than Clorox.

CHAPTER THIRTY-FIVE

Ten minutes later, Mom pulled up to the curb at Fletcher's office and said, "Text when you're finished."

There was no need to text; she never left the parking lot. She was like one of those Little League parents who stayed for practice.

Dr. Fletcher Glasson kept an office in the basement of a large law firm. Right after my first surgery, Dad found Fletcher through my plastic surgeon. He said Dr. Glasson specialized in visual life transitions, and I might benefit from a few sessions.

Benefit was an understatement.

Fletcher was infected with genuine happiness—the kind that couldn't be faked. Which wasn't all that strange except the man had zero reasons for smiles.

He listened to a shit-storm of stories from people like me for a living.

He'd been severely burned in a fire.

Every session gave me hope that maybe someday I'd come out on the other side of my own shit-storm with a smile too.

I clung to that hope. Mondays clearly weren't a busy day at the office. I sat alone with a *People* magazine from a year ago and a *Reader's Digest* from the nineties—both of which I'd already scoured—while the receptionist scrolled through Facebook. Fletcher came around the corner in a matter of moments, smoothing his shirt and stroking his bald head. "Sadie girl," he said, eyes lit with anticipation. "You ready to chat?"

I dropped the magazines and followed.

Seeing the couch opened the portal. His cozy office was as good as an altar and better than a confessional. Fletcher didn't wear a robe or a cross around his neck. In fact, most of the time, he wore faded jeans, deeply colored polo shirts, and a pair of broken-in boots. I had a crush on the boots. And in a very non-crushy way, for the middle-aged man who wore them. Poor bastard, I didn't envy him; his clients walked in and spilled their guts. And Fletcher's job, like a school janitor's, was to spread that sawdust-like absorbent over the guts and sweep them into a pan. Unlike the janitor, Fletcher examined the guts.

One of Fletcher's contagious smiles burned into my eyes as he swiveled his chair away from the desk and faced me. "Sit."

He indicated the couch, as he always did. "Tell me about life."

This was our MO.

I sat. He observed. I talked. He listened.

Then, he questioned me. Gently. Like a nurse who distracts you with stories and lollipops while she gives you a shot in the ass.

I began. "Life's been . . ."

Guts spilled out.

Fletcher spread the vomit-sawdust-stuff over everything between my last visit and now. Gray and Gina's lie. Trent and Callahan. The paintball game. The anniversary. Mom catching me with Sharpies. My fear that Max was the one behind Big's messages. My fear that I was losing Max altogether, messages or not. The incredible shrinking list of impossible things.

When I finally stopped talking, Fletcher leaned forward and rested his hands on his knees. "Well, wasn't that just an emotional enema? I'll bet you feel better already."

"Gross."

He laughed, but it was a serious sort of laugh. "You told me what happened, but not how you feel. You know the rules, Sadie. Go deeper."

I knew the rules because I always tried to break them.

"I'm feeling . . . worried."

"And?"

"Scared."

"And?"

The man was good with his *ands*.

"I don't want to lose Max."

Fletcher passed me the box of tissues he kept on the edge of his desk. I set them down without taking one.

"He feels unreachable," I said. "I screwed up, Fletcher, and . . ."

Worry burrowed under my skin. It had taken me a year to even think about forgiving Gina and Gray; how long would it take Max to forgive me?

I punched the pillow on the couch. "I. Hate. Screwing. Up. I *hate* hurting them. All I wanted to do was put this thing in the past, and now . . . it's messier than ever."

Fletcher examined these guts and forced me to do the same through a series of questions. Always with a smile. Always with compassion. Then, he made a suggestion.

"Sadie, this might be unorthodox, but here's an idea for some common ground. You talked to Gina about the Fountain trip. Why not talk to all of them?"

"You mean ask them to go?"

"Well, it might knock out more than one thing on that list of yours," he said.

"Fletcher, Max isn't answering his phone, and Gray's not going to ride to St. Augustine with me after the paintball fiasco." I shot the guy in the chest at close range.

"You sure about that?"

"Pretty damn."

"Maybe so, but"—Fletcher drummed his fingers on the desk and pushed another button—"if nothing changes, nothing changes. If you keep doing what you're doing, you're going to keep getting what you're getting. You want change, make some."

He made change sound like a Nike slogan. *Just do it.*

It wasn't that easy.

"You seriously want me to ask all three of them to go to the Fountain of Youth?" I asked.

"I *seriously want* you to take a gigantic leap forward. And honestly, when you talk about everything that's happened with your friends over the past week, do you know what I hear?"

"What?"

"Relief." Fletcher whispered the word until it shouted at me. "It's tiny and small, but it's there in your voice for the first time in nearly a year. And you know what, that relief will grow even more when you stop hiding from which *friend* sent the envelopes. Talk to them."

"Who?"

"All of them," he said. "You're strong enough to ask."

Fletcher stared hard at the tissue box, and I surrendered and took one.

"Strength. What a joke. That's what really gets me about this Big thing." I paused to dab my eyes. "This is *someone else* who thinks I'm so frickin' precious that I can't handle the truth. Anonymous letters? Gina and Gray and the Jeep? Dammit, just tell me."

"You say that, but you didn't tell them about Trent. And you don't want to confront Max about Big."

The shovel hit the root.

I tugged the couch pillow into my lap and squeezed it against my chest. "What if I ask, and Max never forgives me? Or, what if I ask, and I never forgive him?"

"Sadie, forgiveness isn't always returning to the old thing. Sometimes forgiveness is making an entirely new thing." Fletcher's watch buzzed that our time was up. "Think about that this week."

"Yeah, I'll do that on my road trip to St. Augustine," I joked.

"You laugh, but it just might happen."

"Yeah, and I might be Miss America."

"You *might*. Lots of cool people have scars."

"Like you," I said, trying to pay him a compliment.

"Like Seal, and Tina Fey, and . . . Jesus."

"That sounds like a really good episode of *Saturday Night Live*."

"I'd watch it." He smiled as I walked to the door. "Last thing before you go." He closed out every session with the same advice. It was his personal mantra, and I loved hearing it. "Scars tell a story, but this week, you decide what that story's going to be."

I hugged the door frame and leaned back into the office. "Hey, Fletcher?"

He stopped fiddling with my folder, where he scratched notes from our session. "Yes, ma'am."

"I want my story to be good."

Dr. Fletcher Glasson smiled a smile worthy of an art exhibit at the Met. "It already is."

CHAPTER THIRTY-SIX

Therapy days were good and bad.

Every time I left Fletcher's I felt like a freshly plowed field. The blades of his words turned soil in my mind, and the process exhausted me. Mom knew. She turned on some folk music and told me to rest. I fell asleep on the five-minute drive.

At home, I showered, stomached a few spoonfuls of peanut butter, and tumbled into bed as if I'd run a marathon rather than spent fifty minutes talking about my life.

Mom and Dad took my naptime by force. The two of them crawled into my king bed in their afternoon sweats. I should have anticipated this. I'd heard Dad call his boss this morning and ask for a personal day. Mom must have canceled all her appointments. They clearly weren't taking any chances I'd emotionally crash after therapy or that I'd located some more Sharpies.

"Seriously?" I said through a curtain of damp hair. "I just got here."

"Scoot over, Sade. You gave us a save-the-date for a movie."

"Don't you two have something better to do?" I teased Dad. "Netflix? Street-sign theft? Or, you know, work?"

"Nope," Mom said. "You want to call Max? We'll move to the living room and make it a party."

I glanced at my phone, which had zero texts or missed calls, and said, "He's doing his own thing today."

Mom parted my hair. "You want me to brush your hair while we watch?"

This offer was a ticket to my soul.

I laid my head on her lap. "What movie did you pick?" Her fingers needled through my hair, and I practically purred.

"Your choice," Dad said. "We've got *Jurassic Park*, *The Breakfast Club*, and *The Empire Strikes Back*."

"Those are all old. I thought we were going to watch something funny."

"Old, schmold, and I beg to differ with your opinions on humor." Dad popped me on the head with the DVD case. "If you make it through any one of them without smiling, I'll grill shrimp for supper."

"Deal. *Jurassic Park*." I snuggled deeper into the bed and Mom's leg. Dad grilled the best shrimp in the world. This was easy eating.

They started the movie. I fell asleep before the first casualty. My dreams were made of dinosaur-people. A T. rex the color of Big sat in the middle of the island, granting life-saving advice through a hole in his claw. He told me I had to drive a car in a tank top or be eaten alive. I ripped the sleeves off my shirt, but when I combed the island for a vehicle, my safari Jeep was a Barbie car with a battery problem. I woke up as the T. rex teeth came at my head.

I noticed the TV was off, Dad was sound asleep, and Mom still fiddled with my hair even though her eyes were closed.

"Bad dream?" she asked as I stirred.

Sleepy me had no filter. I told her all about it.

Her thigh muscles tightened beneath me as she stretched. Her fingers stopped while she yawned.

"Tomorrow, I say, you're going to wear a T-shirt and drive a car."

I lifted my head off her leg. *"Mo-om."*

She just smiled. Our features were similar—full upper lips, wavy blond hair with identical widow's peaks that pointed to crooked button noses, and blue eyes that were occasionally gray. She was beautiful. The way I might have been with some age, had my face not gone through a window.

"Tomorrow. I really believe tomorrow is the day," she said.

"And if I don't?"

"It's not a threat, baby doll. It's a hope."

I relaxed again and she said, "Did you know I've been to El Salvador?"

I didn't. Not once in the entire time the McCalls were gone had she mentioned a visit to Central America. Considering her idea of roughing it was the Hilton, I was shocked she'd even gotten on the plane. If the rest of El Salvador looked like Max's video of the nunnery, my mother had been miserable.

Mom registered my disbelief. "Sonia talked me into it." Huge eye-roll. "It was . . . awful."

We both giggled, but not loud enough to wake Dad. "I mean . . . awful," she continued. "Hot as Hades. I hated the food. Black beans for breakfast. Watered-down beer. It took me thirty minutes to decide I hated it and one day to decide I wanted to go home."

"What'd you do?"

"What do you mean?" she said playfully. "I called my parents, and they changed my plane ticket to the next day."

"For real?"

"Baby, why would I stay somewhere I hated?"

It was such a simple, true statement. I heard it about my life.

If nothing changes, nothing changes.

"You hear me?" she asked.

"Loud and clear."

Mom zippered the conversation closed. "Hey, wake up that bear beside you, and tell him to make us some shrimp."

"But I fell asleep."

"Oh, honey, he was always going to make you shrimp."

After the world's best shrimp, I went for a long run. Eight o'clock. In shorts. Sand kicked up behind me as I rushed mile one and then mile two. Twilight painted the sky purple and orange and gorgeous. I sweated through the layers of my clothes, wishing the last of the sun would fall below the curve, and also that it would stay sunset forever.

I longed to pick a point in the future and transport myself there without having to live all the hard moments in between. I wanted to call my parents and ask them to switch my ticket to a different life.

There wasn't a different ticket, but there were choices. I thought about my conversations with Mom and Fletcher. They, whoever *they* are, say it takes seven times to hear something before it sinks in. For me, it took about seventy billion.

I was finally listening.

I hated this shitty spot with my friends. And why would I stay somewhere I hated?

I wouldn't. Not anymore.

First things first, I sat down in the sand, and rather than write a list, I emailed Max from my phone.

From: sadiemaykingston@gmail.com
To: tothemax@gmail.com
Date: June 26
Subject: I'm SO

Sorry.
I'm sitting out here on the beach thinking about everything that's happened. I'll give you one guess which of these things matters to me most.

A) Trent being gay

B) Gray driving the Jeep

C) Something being off between us

Pick C. I pick C.

Max, I should have told you about Trent a long time ago.

Above me is a sky full of stars. In front of me is an ocean full of waves. Beneath me are a million grains of sand that used to be rock. That ocean I love so much beat rocks into sand. I'm afraid that's what I've done to you. Can you ever forgive me?

I love you, Maxwell Lincoln McCall.

                                        Sadie

He fired an email back almost instantly.

From: tothemax@gmail.com

To: sadiemaykingston@gmail.com

Date: June 26

Subject: It took

Millions of years for that ocean to beat rocks into sand.

We're not that broken.

I love you too, Sadie (May) Elizabeth Kingston.

                                        Max

From: sadiemaykingston@gmail.com

To: tothemax@gmail.com

Date: June 26

Subject: Will you

come over tonight?

From: tothemax@gmail.com

To: sadiemaykingston@gmail.com

Date: June 26

Subject: Of

course.

At eleven that night, Max tapped on my window.

"You're wearing my T-shirt?" he said as he crawled inside.

Tennessee blazed at him, but I willed myself to keep my thoughts elsewhere. Which wasn't hard. Max was shirtless and in a pair of athletic shorts.

"I'm glad you came," I whispered.

"I'm glad you asked."

My eyes drifted to my phone. "Where've you been?"

He faced me. "With Callahan."

Max sat down on the edge of my bed. "Wanna play a game?" he asked, without a hint of play in his voice.

"Something you've never told me?"

He nodded and handed me a creased and grainy photo of a

chalk drawing. The work, if you could call it that, was clearly mine. Before they dismissed me from the hospital, one of the nurses gave me a bucket of sidewalk chalk and told me to use it all before my follow-up appointment. She told me to draw and then hose, draw and then hose—she repeated that more than twice—that the water would wash away more than chalk. She also mentioned, more than twice, that I should trust her.

"I've been giving away chalk buckets for longer than they've made chalk buckets," she'd claimed.

That first week, I had slipped out our back door after midnight and drawn dozens of elementary school–level drawings—emotional outbursts—on our back patio by moon- and streetlight.

"How did you get this?" I asked.

Max didn't answer, and I examined the photo again.

In the middle, there was a crudely drawn caricature of me, lying on my side, a brown-and-gray cape covering me. I'd written *Superhero down* in green chalk. There was a string tied around my pinkie toe that stretched toward a huge peach-colored hand.

Below the hand was another line. *Don't let me go.*

"I love this drawing," Max said, taking it from me and holding it like a talisman. "I snapped a picture before you hosed it off."

"Why would you do that?"

"I was in the hammock when you drew it. You kept repeating a phrase. Do you remember what it was?" he asked.

I didn't remember, but I knew.

"'Hold on. Hold on. Hold on.'"

"That's right," he said. "When you were drawing that, you had steel in your eyes. You had . . . mettle."

"I didn't have a clue."

"You did to me."

"I don't even remember this moment," I admitted.

"You don't have to, because I do. That's when I knew you had pain that looked like mine. We were in that car together. We lost Trent together. I didn't have to go through the rest of life alone."

"You've always seemed like you were okay. Sad, but okay."

"Sadie, I was a thousand miles away. You can't say everything in an email." Max folded his body in half, practically burying his forehead in his knees as he spoke. "There are things I never told you, too. Like . . . I woke up one day in El Salvador, and I couldn't breathe."

He exhaled so hard that it felt as if it bounced off all the walls. "I just lost myself. I took off running, and I ran until I collapsed. I couldn't get back up. My dad found me lying in a street. He carried me back to the compound in his arms."

We were months past this pain in his life, and it sounded as if it had occurred today.

"You could have told me," I whispered.

"I wanted what I gave you to be the good stuff. That's why I disappeared this weekend. Stupid. I was angry and hurt and . . ." He stood up and looked at me and then focused again on the photo. "I forgot how strong you were. I've been forgetting for a while. The picture reminded me."

I wanted to ask about Big. If that's what he meant when he said he'd been forgetting for a while, but I didn't want to ruin this moment.

I chose to say, "You can just be you."

His voice was on the brink and he went back to minimal answers.

"I know."

"How was Callahan?" I asked.

"Happy I knew." Max's eyes misted over. "He loved my brother."

"We all did," I said.

Max pointed to the blanket fort I'd made in the corner of the room, put a finger to his lips, and said, "Let's not talk about Trent right now."

I followed him to the floor and through the entrance.

"You want me to read to you?" I asked.

"Nope."

"You want me to tell you something?"

"Nope," he said. "I want you to tell me everything . . . tomorrow."

I imagined him grinning. I imagined me grinning. I didn't have to imagine us happy, because we already were.

CHAPTER THIRTY-SEVEN

In the early dawn, Max and I whispered back and forth about nothing. Talking about nothing was sometimes better than talking about anything.

"You never told me what your surprise was," I said, poking him awake.

He yawned and asked, "What surprise?"

Even though he knew exactly which surprise. I dug my chin into his chest for teasing me.

"Okay, okay," he said, stroking my back. "I was going to ask if you wanted to go to the Fountain of Youth Park on the anniversary. Thought it might help to get out of town, and I know it's on your list."

Suddenly, it clicked.

"You've been working on my list? Haven't you?"

His hands paused midtouch. "I read your emails over and over. Memorized the things you wanted. Like the tank top and the park. You want to go; just like I know you've been working on driving with Metal Pete."

"How?"

"I asked him."

"You asked Metal Pete?" My voice climbed a ladder.

"Shh, we're going to get caught," he warned. "Yeah. Of course I did. I'd do anything to help."

I tested Fletcher's idea on him.

"What do you think about the four of us going?" I asked.

Silence.

More silence.

"Max?"

"If that's what you want, let's do it," he said.

"You hesitated."

"Five or so hours in the car with Gray—" he said.

"Ten or so hours," I corrected, since we had to also drive home. "And I'm not sure I can do it either. I'm not even sure he'll agree."

"Well, I'll bring the paintball gun just in case," he said. "I've heard that works pretty well."

Neither of us laughed. "That was a mistake. I shouldn't have shot him."

"He told you to."

"That doesn't make it right. But maybe this will."

"For your sake, I hope he says yes."

★ ★ ★

Later on in the day, long after Max slipped out my window, Gina and Gray agreed to meet Max and me at the Salvage Yard on the morning of the anniversary. Two days from now.

That meant I had work to do.

I showed up at Metal Pete's with two bags of doughnuts and two choices of coffee, still wearing Max's T-shirt to channel my brave. Surely caffeine and sugar would woo Metal Pete into submission, and the T-shirt would prove I was serious about change.

I walked toward the office feeling hopeful.

Metal Pete eyed me suspiciously when I set the morning feast on his desk. "You're . . . up to something," he said. "Spill the beans."

"That car you promised me," I began.

Metal Pete began most expressions with a scrunched nose and raised eyebrows. This one ended up in a smile. "Uh-huh?" he said.

I gave him a prize-winning grin. "Could I maybe borrow that on Thursday?"

"You mean you want to drive it off the lot?"

I nodded.

"Like . . . you're going to take the car through the gate, hit the gas, and put it on an actual road and . . . ?"

His skepticism wasn't a refusal. It was a challenge.

"Somehow. Some way," I said, even though I wasn't quite sure of that part myself.

"And where might you be taking this borrowed car of mine?"

"St. Augustine."

"St. *Augustine*?" he practically screamed. "Whoa, kid. You don't start small, do you?"

"I'm just glad to finally be starting," I told him.

Metal Pete strolled over to a gray box that hung on his wall and examined rows and rows of keys. He settled on one, and said, "Follow me."

Together, we walked down the first row of cars. I had never spent much time in this row. The cars here were all in good shape. Good being a relative thing: most people wouldn't look twice at them, but I wasn't most people. I eyed an old black Trans-Am and crossed my fingers. It was a car that screamed Road Trip, and it was much bigger than the Yaris.

But Metal Pete walked past the Trans-Am and stopped at a little red S-10 extended cab. His hand caressed the bed as if the old Chevrolet were a woman he loved.

"Not putting you in a car," he said matter-of-factly. "Rebuilt this engine myself. It's the best I've got. Plus, it's insured."

Don't cry. Don't cry, I thought as I considered Pete's generosity. "Pete . . ."

"Nope," Pete warned. He took my hand the way my grandfather had when I was a little girl. Squeezing it once, he said, "I won't have any of that sap. You're not a tree."

The keys were in my hand then.

"You've got two days to prove to me you can do it," he told

me, and opened the door with a bow.

"I won't be going alone," I promised him.

"Naw, I didn't figure you were."

I climbed in and rolled down the window. Moment of truth. Sweat lined the creases of my hands as I turned the key.

The engine didn't argue.

Quickly, before I changed my mind, I tapped the brake and shifted into reverse. The trucked rolled slowly backward, and I watched everything. The parked row of cars behind me. Metal Pete, smiling under his visor. My own nervous face in the rear-view.

Nervous or not, I had the truck in drive.

"That's it, kid," Metal Pete yelled as I turned the wheel at the end of the row.

Driving wasn't all that hard. Everything from my months of training with Mom and Dad came back in that first lap around the row. I could have walked faster than I was driving, but I knew, even at ten miles per hour, that *not* driving was just another one of those things I'd built into a fortress of impossibility. After I took a few loops around the rows, I shifted to neutral, and wrote the original list in the dashboard dust.

1. Wear a tank top in public *(Check-ish)*

2. Walk the line at graduation *(Not yet)*

3. Forgive Gina *(Check)* and Gray *(Not checked)*. *And* tell them the truth. *(Double check)*

4. Stop following. Start leading. *(?—If I pulled this off)*

5. Drive a car again *(Bonus points)*

6. Kiss someone without flinching *(Hell yeah)*

7. Visit the Fountain of Youth *(Maybe Thursday)*

Holy wow, this was serious progress. Feeling slightly confident from my successes, I added one more thing:

8. Confront Gray *and Max* about Big

Number eight needed to be on the list, regardless of the consequences. I finally knew I was strong enough to handle the truth, even if it was Max. I wanted it to be Gray, but I had a gut feeling it wasn't. This had not been a year of getting what I wanted.

I drove cautiously back to Metal Pete, honking the S-10's horn as I approached.

When I put the truck in park, Metal Pete leaned through the window, his eyes moist with pride. "You look like an old pro out there."

"Yeah, a regular NASCAR goddess," I joked. "I need to do this."

"You *need* to try it on the real road. The interstate is a far cry from the yard."

Fear descended on me.

Metal Pete turned his head and whistled. From under one of the old school buses, Headlight appeared. She loped lazily for two steps and then broke into a full gallop toward the truck.

"Take Headlight here over to Ferry Park and let her run around," Metal Pete said. He gave me the assignment the same way he'd sent me on scavenger hunts in the Yard, with the confidence that I could do anything.

I leaned across the cab and opened the door. Without being told, Headlight hopped onto the bench beside me and lay her head down on my lap. Her foxlike ears pointed at the sky as Pete told her to be good for me.

"I'll be right back," I told him.

He nodded. "Call if you get stuck." He tapped the hood twice, granting permission for me to leave.

I had to call.

I had to call the next day too.

The road and I were not yet friends, but we had more than ten hours on Thursday to get acquainted.

CHAPTER THIRTY-EIGHT

Some Emails to Max in El Salvador

From: sadiemaykingston@gmail.com

To: tothemax@thecenter.es

Date: May 29

Subject: One year

Max,

One month from today it will be a year.

Love,

Sadie

From: sadiemaykingston@gmail.com

To: tothemax@thecenter.es

Date: May 29
Subject: RE: One year

Max,
No, I think we should do something he'd love.

<3
Sadie

From: sadiemaykingston@gmail.com
To: tothemax@thecenter.es
Date: May 29
Subject: RE: cemetery visit?

Max,
Honestly, I haven't been back to the cemetery. I haven't driven
by the scene. I haven't even been out to see the plaque they
put up at Coast Memorial. But if you want to go, I will go with
you.

Love,
Sadie

From: sadiemaykingston@gmail.com
To: tothemax@thecenter.es
Date: May 29
Subject: Willit Hill

Max,

It's not the places that scare me. It's letting him go. That
sounds so stupid, because I know he's already gone. But he
isn't. Not to me.

                                        Love,
                                        Sadie

From: sadiemaykingston@gmail.com
To: tothemax@thecenter.es
Date: May 29
Subject: the music of Trent

Max,

I miss his voice. I wish I didn't have that "Hold on. Hold on.
Hold on" chorus in my head.

                                        Love,
                                        Sadie

From: sadiemaykingston@gmail.com
To: tothemax@thecenter.es
Date: May 29
Subject: <333

Max,

I'm sure your call cost a million dollars, but for tonight, I have your sweet voice stuck in my head now. This year took away many things, but it was generous, too. I have you, and I'll never be sorry about that.

<3 <3 <3

Sadie

CHAPTER THIRTY-NINE

The morning of the anniversary I woke up with a tank on my chest and shrapnel in my brain.

I'd spent most of the night flipping over and over in bed, unsettled and restless, so tired my eyes wouldn't close. Four hundred games of phone solitaire later, I'd fallen asleep and awakened with a jolt an hour later. Anticipation and sleep were sworn enemies.

I turned on the light, thinking I might read. With all my tossing and turning, I'd knocked Big out of the bed. When I leaned over to pick him up, a piece of paper fell out.

Gray Garrison is my one true love.

The timing on that one was from early sophomore year.

I remembered how sharp and focused that feeling had been. He'd sent me a whole bunch of YouTube links to *Peter and the Starcatcher*. It wasn't a huge gift; it was the way he understood me and my passions.

Gray had agreed to go road-tripping with me today for the same reason.

I removed the next piece from Big and then the next and the next until he was empty, and I'd worn memory lane into a dirt path.

These paper memories were a time machine, but they weren't for a time I wanted to revisit. I'd come through them, and I didn't want to go back. Because Gray's vase was a relic from the same time period, I put the papers inside and set Big on my shelf, not quite ready to let an old friend go. It felt wrong to keep the vase in my room, so I padded down the hallway to the closet and put it inside.

That wasn't far enough away. I wanted the papers gone-gone, and I knew the perfect place to put them.

Even though it was four in the morning, I walked outside in my bare feet, clutching the vase, and started the scooter. The drive to the foot of Willit Hill took me ten minutes.

No one had ever put up a cross or a sign that said what happened here, but the pine trees bore the evidence. Even the trees had scars. I froze on the side of the road, realizing I hadn't been back here in a year.

Mom had avoided this road.

Dad had avoided this road.

I had avoided this road.

I wasn't avoiding it anymore. I left the scooter by the rumble strip and hiked down to the site of the accident, the ground punishing my feet. Balancing myself against the tree, I kneeled down as if I were in a cemetery, and I talked to Trent.

"It's been a year. It's been a really hard year without you. Losing you felt like jumping off the bridge and forgetting which way was up. I don't think I'll ever be over it, but I'm starting to find my way through it. Mom said when a person dies, you don't get over it by forgetting; you get through it by remembering. I've been remembering everything lately.

"I told Max and Gray and Gina about you. They're dealing. And you know, I think they would have dealt if you'd told them. You were worried about that, but they love you. Same as me. Max even spent some time with Chris. I thought you'd want to hear that. I've spent a lot of time trying to find myself. Exploring. You were supposed to be with me for searches like that. Sometimes I can't handle the injustice that you're not. Sometimes, I stand still while the world moves. You'd hate it. You'd hate this version of me.

"So I want you to know . . . today, I'm starting over. Without you.

"I'm going to leave something to keep you company. You were the first one to stuff a fortune inside Big. And practically everything in him is what you loved about me and our friends.

I'm going to leave them here, with you."

I dug down into the pile of pine needles and made a place for the vase.

I covered it up with needles.

I covered it up with tears.

And I told my friend good-bye.

When I listened for his voice, for that chorus of last words, there was only silence.

I guess he'd finally said good-bye too.

The stars were still out as I climbed the ditch to the Spree. I gazed up at the constellations, allowing myself a moment of observation and, perhaps, hesitation. I remembered a conversation Trent and I had when we were kids.

He'd just come back from space camp in Huntsville, and we were lying on the dock for an hour of Star Time.

"Sadie, did you know we can see nineteen trillion miles with our eyes? Nineteen trillion miles."

This clearly impressed him. He went on about it, pointing out the stars and telling how far they were from Earth. One week at space camp hardly made him an expert, but he didn't know that.

Space camp or no, I wanted to show him it mattered to me. That I'd done my own space camp that week with Google and books from the library.

"Cool. Watch this," I told him.

I lifted my thumb into the air, closed my left eye, and made Orion disappear. "Did you know Neil Armstrong did this after he got into space?"

"Did what? Gave Earth a thumbs-up?" he asked, interested.

I loved that I knew something he didn't.

"Yeah, so Armstrong said he realized that from where he was in space he could lift his thumb into the air and make all of Earth disappear. He said he didn't feel like a giant, though. I read it in a book while you were gone."

Trent lifted his thumb into the air, closed one eye, and blocked out the Big Dipper.

"Crazy," he said. "Sometimes a small thing is bigger than a big thing."

The wisdom of Neil Armstrong, Star Time, and a thirteen-year-old came back to me as I stared up at a perfect sky, balanced with equal parts light and dark.

I held my thumb out to the past until I couldn't see it anymore, and then I drove home.

Sometimes a small thing is bigger than a big thing.

I'd just done a small thing.

CHAPTER FORTY

Max knocked on my window at six thirty a.m.

I'd come home from Willit Hill and napped.

"Hop to it, Kingston," Max told me when I raised the window a crack.

"I'm coming. I'm coming."

I rushed around for five minutes doing the necessary things—like putting on clean underwear and deodorant, and packing essentials—and five minutes doing totally unnecessary things, like changing clothes and hairstyles several times. I shoved Big, what was left of him, deep in my bag.

"We're not going to the third world," Max said from his perch in the window when he saw my bag.

"Cut me some slack. I rarely leave my street."

He kissed my cheek and said, "Speaking of. You'd better

tell them"—he pointed toward my parents' room—"where we're going."

I wrote Mom and Dad a note that could warrant either a high five or a *What the hell?* and left it on the bar. They wanted my driving status out of neutral, but St. Augustine wasn't exactly one city over. As far as they knew, I hadn't even made it to the bridge by myself, and that was only down the street. So in a moment of overkill, I added a big smiley face to sell them on my mental state.

I'm happy. I'm good with this. I can drive ten hours round-trip.

I expected a phone call in T-minus soon.

As Max and I drove the Spree down our street, the first hint of sunbeams struck the pale-gray sky in a brilliant effort. The houses glowed like color cards at a paint store in shades of peach, tan, blue, and aquamarine. There was a white stucco house shaped like a dome that had been rebuilt several times. Some places still had blue tarps secured to the roof with two-by-fours, the aftermath of the storm that tackled the dome.

But they were all still here.

So was I.

And in a few minutes, I'd sit behind the wheel and drive to St. Augustine. When I was a kid, I marveled at airplanes and space shuttles. I watched fighter jets from Eglin Air Force Base run routes out to sea, leaving white traceable contrails against bright blue skies. Dad had even taken me to Cape Canaveral once to watch a launch. Those crafts seemed like impossibilities hurling through space. Cars had never dazzled me. They didn't look like miracles with their wheels, engines, and speed. They were made of logic.

Until the accident.

Every day, the people around me got into vehicles and hurled their bodies down the road at high speeds. Didn't they know that more people died in cars than in airplanes? Didn't they know Trent was one of them? That Max and I almost were? I didn't think they did. They texted and talked on the phone and ate take-out and changed their iPods from one song to another.

Driving needed a little more formal dining room and a little less backyard toy box. That fear was what started me running. My feet felt pretty damn safe.

But I couldn't walk to St. Augustine.

"You're quiet," Max said.

"So are you."

"Might be a quiet sort of day," he said.

Gina and Gray were parked outside Metal Pete's gate when we arrived. I'd left it to Gina to explain the day to Gray, and she'd promised me he was on board. We greeted one another cautiously. There was none of the humor of chicken-fighting and camping as we walked into the yard.

"Why can't we just go in Gina's car?" Gray asked.

"Because I want to drive."

Everyone stopped in the middle of the dirt lane. Even Max.

"Why did you think we were here?" I said, jangling the keys as I walked my friends down the first row toward the S-10.

"No idea," Gray said.

"Ritual," Max said cautiously.

I read his mind. He clearly thought I was making the other two see the Yaris before we drove off together.

"I've been practicing." I left out the *for two days* part.

Gina wrapped me up in a hug and said, "You *can* do this."

"Thanks, buddy," I said, allowing the praise to give me courage.

My practicing didn't seem to quell Gray's or Max's fears. The discomfort amped up again when I showed them the extended-cab truck that was our vehicle for the day.

"You want us to ride in *that* for ten—" Gray stopped himself.

If the tone had been lighter and the circumstances had been a little different, his agitation would have been funny. Here and now, it annoyed me, and he knew it. The four of us climbed into the truck, Max and me in the front, Gina and Gray facing each other in the back. The space was so tight, their knees touched. When I fastened my seat belt, Max checked on me.

You okay? he mouthed.

A posse ad esse, I mouthed back.

He nodded, and I turned the key.

"You guys ready?" I asked.

No one answered. Verbally or nonverbally. No one breathed when I backed out of the space. As I put the truck in drive, it felt as if someone had tied my throat in a knot. A cold bead of sweat slipped down my back. My knees trembled so fiercely, I was terrified to take my foot off the brake.

Gray was the one who broke my panic. He leaned into the space between the two headrests and said, "God, I hope no one *needs* Gina's tires or hubcaps while we're gone."

We all laughed nervously, and I put my foot on the gas.

CHAPTER FORTY-ONE

Driving was much harder to do when other cars (that moved) were involved and there was an audience. By the time I got to the I-10 ramp, I still hadn't gone more than forty-five miles per hour, and no one had said a word.

Max occupied himself by drumming out rhythms on the window. Gina sang along to the radio, and Gray sat so close to the window that I couldn't see him in the rearview, which was probably a good thing. Mostly, I gripped the steering wheel for dear life and prayed every prayer I knew. Fear was awkward. It was hard to be scared of something that everyone else was comfortable with.

"You'll have to go faster on the interstate," Max said carefully.

I knew that.

I just didn't know if I could.

Every time I accelerated, we lurched forward so fast that I took my foot off the pedal altogether. With all the starts and stops, we moved like a broken ride at the county fair.

"I'll try," I told him.

Mom chose that moment to call.

"Want me to answer?" Max asked.

I nodded, and he rummaged through my bag until he found my phone in the bottom. His eyebrows rose at the sight of Big. On what must have been the last ring, he hit the button and said, "Hi, Mrs. Kingston. This is Max."

Mom said something. I couldn't hear what, but Max told her, "She's driving right now."

I heard her squeal. Bad squeal? Good squeal? Angry squeal? I didn't dare take my eyes off the road to see Max's response.

A semi roared by me, shaking the truck. Behind the semi, a woman driving a Hummer laid on the horn and jerked into the middle lane.

"Shit. People are crazy," I yelled.

Max cupped the phone. "Your mom says, 'Language.'"

I exhaled a very weak laugh, and drove over the rumble strip and into the emergency lane. Releasing the wheel wasn't easy. My knuckles ached with the strain of the few miles we'd traveled.

Max handed me the phone. "Hi, Mom," I said, once I had my voice at an even keel.

"Sadie, where are you guys?"

"On I-10."

Because my mom was terrible at whispering, I heard her repeat this to Dad. He was equally bad, so I heard my dad say, "Ask her if she's okay."

"I'm fine," I said.

Saying it almost convinced me.

"You're sure?"

"Honey"—Mom's voice was made of rainbows and puppies—"we're proud of you for doing this."

Whoa. Off-script. Weren't they required by parental law to say they were worried and ground me for trying something so ridiculous and dangerous? Two days ago, I'd been selfish and rude for going off on my own. Two days ago, I'd been sent to therapy.

"I . . ." Didn't know what to say.

Mom continued. "Call if you need us."

"O-kay," I said.

She hung up.

I stared out the window. Dust stirred and cotton fields rose up like seas of cumulus clouds. Azaleas the size of mobile homes waved in the breeze.

The azaleas jogged the memory of Trent and me lying in a field, talking about things that mattered.

"I want to matter. I want *this* to matter," I told the group.

They all nodded.

Even though we were a long way from St. Augustine—especially if I never drove more than forty-five miles an hour—I eased the truck toward a rest area. When we were parked, I told Gina, Gray, and Max the whole story of Trent and Callahan. Gray wondered if Trent was ever attracted to him. I told Gray no, not that I knew of. Gina asked if Callahan loved him. Max answered that with a resounding yes. Max said how we all felt: some people are hard to understand and easy to love. That was Trent.

That was all of us.

"Why didn't we do *this* a year ago?" Gray asked.

Max had an answer. "We were all in different places then."

I added to it. "We were different people."

"I guess we were," Gray said.

Gina nudged my arm. "We should get on the road. You still okay?"

To answer her, I reversed from the parking spot and headed toward the ramp with increased speed in mind. Ten miles per hour. Twenty. Thirty. Forty.

Max sighted the traffic for me. "You can get over."

I followed his voice onto the interstate.

Fifty.

Fifty-five.

I thought my heart might explode.

Sixty.

Sixty-five.

Max watched the needle climb. "Hit the cruise," he said.

Cruise. (n.) my first successful drive on I-10.

CHAPTER FORTY-TWO

We got gas in Tallahassee, and I took a ten-minute walk to settle down and stretch. By Jacksonville, my frazzled nerves sat on the end of their ends.

I was so close—forty-one miles, according to the signs on the interstate—I could practically taste Ponce's magic spring water. Those forty-one miles might as well have been a thousand. We holed up in a McDonald's parking lot, eating french fries, sweating, and avoiding the obvious problem.

"Will one of you drive?" I finally asked.

"I'll do it," Gray said quietly.

I felt his hesitation and his courage. The last time he'd driven somewhere when we were all involved was a year ago. Maybe he needed to get behind the wheel as badly as I had. Maybe he just wanted out of the cramped backseat.

We played musical chairs, swapping places in the truck. Gina and I were snug in the back, even though my legs were not nearly as long as Gray's.

Max amped the radio and turned on a playlist he'd made of Trent's favorite songs as we pulled out of McDonald's. Amos Lee, Ben Howard, the Head and the Heart. Music was a two-way street where nearly everyone traveled. Those songs were more than music; they were good memories. As Gray drove east, I rested my head against the side glass and let the motion of the highway thrum through my body like the songs.

Somewhere on the outskirts of St. Augustine, Max slid his hand backward between the seat and the door. As I reached for his fingers, a glare of white greeted me from his passenger side door pocket. Envelopes. At least three of them. I couldn't be sure they had my name on the front, but I suspected they did.

I curled my hand into his, eyes still on the envelopes, heart still curious. Max turned in his seat, a smile on his face, and invited me into a whisper.

I brought my ear as close to his mouth as I could. "You did great at driving. I'm really glad we came on this trip," he said.

"Me too."

When he turned around, I slid the envelopes into my bag.

Gina saw me do it, raised her eyebrows, and nodded toward the front seat.

Toward Max?

Toward Gray?

At this point, I didn't want it to be either of them.

CHAPTER FORTY-THREE

Gray braked and wound through the streets of St. Augustine. The oldest town in the United States wore its age like a classic movie star. As we neared the inlet, Gray lowered his window and warm, salty air filled the cab.

He pulled into the parking lot of the Fountain of Youth Archaeological Park and announced, "We're here. Man, I'll bet old Poncey wished there'd been a sign like this back in the day."

Trent would have said the same thing. I realized Gray had been trying to fill in Trent's gaps for a while.

Gina clinched my knee and smiled before I climbed out of the truck. The bright afternoon sunshine forced me to grab a straw hat to add to my sunglasses. I glanced in the mirror and harnessed my courage. Slipping off the long-sleeve shirt, I exposed Tennessee and the *Peter and the Starcatcher* T-shirt

Gray had bought for my sixteenth birthday. It had been my swimsuit cover-up a year ago today. I'd found it in the hall closet this morning, where Mom and Dad had stowed the stuff they'd removed from the Yaris.

"Nice shirt," Gray said as he walked by toward the ticket counter.

Max beamed and tugged on the short sleeve. "Good for you."

Gina stayed close as the boys wandered toward the sign. She helped me lather special SPF into my pallid skin and said, "You're going to get some extra vitamin D today."

I tossed the sunscreen into the truck. "Gotta start somewhere."

Gina spun in a loose circle, taking in as much of the park as she could see from the parking lot. "I can't believe we're actually here."

Our trip had been a year in the making. We were four instead of five, but we were here. "We made it," I said.

Gray heard me. He shook the fatigue from his legs and stretched toward the sky, rolling his thick neck in a circle. "Thank God. World's longest trip."

Gina came to my defense. "It wasn't that bad."

Both Max and Gray laser-eyed her, and she corrected. "It was long, but it wasn't bad."

Gray tried again. "World's longest year?"

"Amen," we all said at once.

Luckily, the park didn't appear too busy. Only a handful of

THE LIES ABOUT TRUTH

vehicles were in the lot. The high humidity had probably sent tourists and visiting families to the mall or the movies. At the ticket counter, each of us forked over the price of admission. Eyeing our water bottles as if they were vermin, the counter lady handed us a park map and a coupon for some genuine Fountain of Youth water.

"Have a nice day," she told us.

Told us. She wasn't a lady who made suggestions.

"Back at you," Gray said jovially.

Then he turned to us and said, "That old gal needs to drink a gallon by herself."

"That's what people probably say about me," I muttered.

Max's head tilted and his eyes grew sad at my self-deprecation. "Not today." He tapped the front of my hat. "You look great."

I ducked my head and pocketed the receipt, unsure of what to say. Reflexively, Gina slipped her arm through mine. I wondered how much she knew about the envelopes. Did everyone know except me? Could Max and Gray have sent them together, and that's why she nodded toward the front of the truck, rather than to one side or the other? I hadn't considered that possibility before.

If my mind was in darkness, hers had both feet anchored to light.

"We should skip," she said, chin up, decision already made.

"Skip?" I asked.

"It's the Fountain of frickin' Youth. Come on."

Gray cut his eyes at Max. "If you want to skip, you're shit out of luck."

Gina didn't wait on me to agree. She tugged my arm and body along for a ride until we skipped and smiled and were young girls again.

I could half see us ten years ago with pigtails and cotton dresses on the playground at Coastal Elementary, eating Lunchables and talking about how stupid the boys were. That was back when we said things like *You'll be my best friend forever and ever and ever and ever. No matter what.*

We'd believed it then.

I started to believe it again.

After we passed through the archway entrance, fifteen acres of green space, statues, forts, and artifacts stretched out in front of us. Somewhere beyond them was the bay where Ponce de Leon had landed in search of gold and a legend. Not far from us now was the old Spring House, which sheltered the Fountain of Youth. For something I'd waited so long to see, it felt a great deal like other parks I'd visited. Part of me expected to see grandparent-aged children frolicking through Roman-style marble baths.

I wasn't sure where to start, but everyone looked at me to decide.

"Spring House?" Max asked.

I hesitated. "Let's save that until last."

"Statue?" Gray asked, but he'd already started in the direction of the old conquistador.

Gina let go of me and caught up with him. Likewise, Max settled into the space beside me. We wandered along the paved paths and sometimes off them. I allowed myself the freedom to feel everything and remember whatever I wanted, like a parade marching through my brain.

Gina. Skipping. With her arm looped through mine.

Gray. The vase of history I'd buried in the pine needles.

Big. An empty stuffed ostrich.

The anniversary. Today.

The list. Shrinking.

Max. Invader. Explorer. Culprit?

When I looked up, the golden statue of Ponce, mounted on a large stone base, loomed over me. I stood in the conquistador's shadow and imagined him landing here for the first time.

The early explorers were cruel and ruthless. They were also brave sons of bitches. I envied the hell out of them for their small Earth and expanding maps. What was left to discover these days? Fashion trends and the next social media quick fix?

As I stared up at that big statue, I wondered how long it had taken him to get his land legs back under him after his voyage. Did he kiss the ground and thank God and the king for traveling mercies? Did he look for an immediate fight with the natives? Or did he wonder the same thing I was wondering now?

Was there really healing in all this water?

"What do you think Trent would have said?" I asked Gina.

"Probably something like 'Sadie May, what shall we

explore next? Machu Picchu? Angkor Wat?'"

Her impression was dead-on.

"You nailed that."

"I knew him pretty well."

She did. I was glad she remembered that.

"He'd have laughed when I told him those places were a long way away."

She tilted her head to the sky. "I can almost hear him."

I thought I could too.

Max chimed in. "The height and depth and width of the universe—how immeasurable it was—always energized him. I wish he'd had a chance to travel."

Even that sounded more like Trent than Max. No one added to his statement. We drifted away from one another. Drifted into our memories.

Someone touched my shoulder.

"It's just me," Max said, jumping back as I jerked.

"Can we talk?" I asked.

"I was coming to ask you the same thing," he said.

I consulted the park map and yelled to Gina and Gray that Max and I were walking toward Ponce's landing spot. He slipped his hand into mine.

I wondered if we'd ever walk this way again.

I hoped we would.

I'd forgiven Gina. Gray and I had been civil all day. I could forgive Max if I needed to. Right?

When we were bayside, I chose a bench and sat down

cross-legged, facing sideways. The sun-heated wood warmed my skin through my jeans. Max sat across from me. Sweat gathered in the edges of his sideburns. It was pretty damn hot out here, I thought, tugging at the middle of my shirt.

"I wanted to tell you I'm sorry," he said, and then clarified. "That I doubted we should all come here. This was a good choice. You've wanted to forgive them, and this is a huge step in that direction."

I couldn't hold on to the words any longer. "I saw the envelopes in the truck."

He flipped his hat from backward to forward—his eyes disappearing as he wiggled in his seat. "What envelopes?"

I shuffled through my bag and placed all three in front of him. As if the action itself would demand a response.

Max scooted back into the armrest, picked up the one on top, and read my name. "Sadie Kingston."

Before I drew a conclusion, someone behind me spoke.

"It wasn't him."

My hand found its way to my mouth. *Gray.*

"I'm really confused," Max said.

"No, I was really confused," I said. "Gray—"

"Made another mistake," he filled in. Gray gave Max a sympathetic look. "She'll explain it all to you soon, Max. Would you mind maybe giving us a minute alone?"

Max looked as confused as I felt. Still, he stood, respecting Gray's request.

I grabbed Max's hand.

He double-squeezed. "It's okay." Then he winked, and walked away.

Gray took his place on the bench.

We let our hearts speak one-on-one.

His heart: "I sent them because I didn't know what else to do. You wouldn't hear me."

My heart: "I wasn't ready. I *couldn't* hear you."

His heart: "I thought you might hear yourself."

My heart: "I wish you'd signed them."

His heart: "If you'd known it was me, you would have thrown them away."

My heart: "I guess you're right."

His heart: "Sadie . . . did they help at all?"

My heart: "In the craziest way, yes. The past wasn't all bad, was it?"

He knew the answer to that question. It was one of the things he'd held on to with an iron grip. It was why he'd sent the envelopes.

My heart: "I'd forgotten that."

His heart: "Then I'm glad I reminded you."

More followed. Why he'd chosen those particular memories. How he'd done it. For a laugh, he and Trent had gone through Big during last year's Pirates and Paintball.

"You always told us they weren't really secrets. Our curiosity got the better of us," he said guiltily. "I really liked the stuff you wrote. The little pieces of us you captured."

He explained how he and Trent had taken phone shots of

a few—some he'd loved, like us jumping off the bridge, and a few he'd hated, like me and Trent skinny-dipping.

"Your gun didn't misfire at Pirates and Paintball, did it?" I asked, remembering that Trent had been on our team last year and Gray had been the one to *accidentally* shoot him in the face mask.

Gray gave me a solemn nod. "Reading that made me furious. He didn't have any right to see you naked before I did."

"Just so you know, he never saw me naked."

Gray sighed. "It's not like it would have mattered if he had—not now—but I didn't know that then. End of the day, I used all the memories, because all those slips added up to the girl I fell in love with, and I missed her."

I teared up when Gray explained how the idea of sending the letters came to him. He'd been sitting across the street from my house missing me. Worried about me.

"I saw you there," I told him.

"Probably not. It was early," he said.

"It was right at sunrise." The image of him squatting on the curb, underneath my mailbox, sharpened in my mind. "You were wearing a light gray hoodie, the one I used to steal, and jeans."

I'd written to Max about seeing him.

"I guess you did." Gray inched closer, and opened his palm. I lay my hand on top of his.

"You were hurting, Sade. Shutting down. Withdrawing. I had to do something to reach you, and it was the best I could think of. Honestly, I was kind of proud of myself for doing something Trent would have done."

Gray was right. From the very beginning, the letters had reminded me of Trent, which is ultimately why I'd suspected Max instead of Gray. Gray Garrison still had surprises up his sleeve. That made me happy for him and whoever came after me.

"You could have told me on the beach. The day I helped you put up chairs. Or at paintball. Or anytime."

"Would we be here right now if I had?" he asked quietly.

I guess we both knew the answer to that.

Gray Garrison leaned forward and said, "Even if you hate me, seeing you drive, seeing you take off those damn long sleeves, seeing you here"—he looked around—"that was worth it for me."

"I don't hate you, Gray."

"I meant what I said. I still love you, Sadie."

In a weirdly mistaken, human way, he'd more than demonstrated that.

I tiptoed through the minefield carefully. Clocks didn't run in reverse, and neither could we.

"Gray." My voice fell heavy between us. "I still care about you, too—"

He retracted his hand. "But—"

"The past has to stay the past," I said. "And not because you cheated on me. Because we changed, and that's okay."

A chorus of ghostly hands clapped when I said that. It felt

like we'd come to the end of a long amusement park ride. I imagined an announcer speaking into a shoddy microphone. *Ladies and gentlemen, carefully unbuckle your seat belts and exit to the left. Thank you for riding the End of Us.*

Gray scratched his head and closed his eyes. For once, I knew he wasn't closing out the picture of me. He was closing out the picture of us.

"I really thought we'd make it," he said.

"We did. Just not in the way we thought we would."

"True," he said.

"True," I said.

The truth was finally a beautiful thing.

CHAPTER FORTY-FOUR

Gina and Max must have been watching us. The moment we stood, they arrived, map out, ready to explore.

"Want to check out the Spring House?" I asked, my voice nearly normal.

"Absolutely," Gina said.

"Anywhere you want to go," Max said.

I took Max's hand, hoping he'd accept mine, hoping he understood that true closure had happened with Gray. He did, spinning his hat around backward, the way I loved, and rubbing the scruffy part of his chin against my face to make me laugh. Some people just snapped back into place. Thank the good Lord for the occasional easy answer.

Gray moved closer to Gina, but not so close as to make a

statement. "Let's go drink Ponce's Kool-Aid," he said.

We all laughed.

The Spring House was near the park entrance and a short walk from the statue. Other than the two wire peacocks that flanked the sign, the doorway looked like a hobbit hole. It looked like comfort.

"Sadie, I think we've found the Shire," Max teased.

"Cross it off your list," I said.

Sharing a heart with someone isn't a crowded thing when they understand you that well. I squeezed his hand, trying to tell him that without words, and Max got it loud and clear.

The earthen room we entered wasn't grand. It had Dixie cups and a semi-hokey museum display. Six-year-old Sadie would have loved it with her whole heart.

Gray said, "Seriously? This is it?"

Gina shoved him toward the door and he said, "I'm kidding. It's great."

I sort of doubted that was true.

The sound of water hitting water captured our attention. Not the roar of a waterfall, but a dime-size stream that fell into a tiny well.

I watched it without speaking.

I stepped away from Max, closed one eye, and held up my thumb until it blocked the small fountain.

"Neil Armstrong," Max said.

I smiled.

"Trent told me."

Sometimes a small thing was bigger than a big thing.

Gina and Gray watched curiously, but didn't ask what we were doing. Gray stepped forward and took two Dixie cups from the table and filled them up.

"We should toast," Gina said.

Max filled two cups for us and we made a semicircle.

"To Trent," Max said.

"To Trent," we said together, knocking the plastic cups against one another.

Cold and good. Healing? We'd see.

"To us," I said.

"To us," my friends said.

That drink tasted like the first day of autumn. Cool. Refreshing. Like water from a garden hose, except without the metallic after-bite. I felt as if I'd arrived at the end of a long journey.

Friendship was more of an adventure than we intended for it to be. Maybe it was Ponce's magic fountain. Maybe it was Sadie Kingston growing a freaking brain and a pair of cojones. I'd been waiting for a feeling and had gotten it backward. The feeling had been waiting for me. Choosing forgiveness takes more courage (and far less energy) than sustaining anger.

I decided.

Forgiveness (n.) releasing the toxins of bitterness.

Tears fell from my eyes as I said the two words I'd withheld, though they'd been given to me many times this year.

"I'm sorry," I told them.

And to be sure they understood, I got specific, starting with Gina and Gray. "I shut both of you out, because you were in the front car . . . because . . . I blamed you. I thought you couldn't understand, and really, I didn't understand, or even acknowledge, what you'd been through either. I'm sorry we didn't talk. Sorry for my anger. Sorry I pretended to sleep when you visited. I pushed you away. I pushed you together."

"Sadie." Gina tried to stop me.

"We still messed up," Gray said.

"You've given me a year of apologies; I still owe you a few more," I said.

They nodded and slid closer together.

Max placed his hand on the small of my back, and as I continued, I inched toward his strength. "Guys, I'm sorry you felt like you couldn't tell me the truth. And that all those times when you apologized, I wasn't listening. We lost Trent together, and I'm sorry it took me a year to start healing. And Max . . ."

"Hey, we're good," he said.

"We *are* good," I said with a slight grin. "But I should have Skyped with you. Should have shown who I was and trusted you to see me the way you do. I was scared I'd lose you, too."

He shrugged, as if it was no big deal. "I get to see you now every day. We're all better than we were."

"Hear, hear," Gina said.

"Hear, hear," we all echoed.

No blubber sessions followed. No conversations. We all filled up another cup and chugged.

CHAPTER FORTY-FIVE

Outside the Spring House, the sun scorched us. I lowered my sunglasses and squinted at Gray, who pointed in the direction of the gift shop. Woe to us if we didn't commemorate the experience with a souvenir magnet.

Max used the coupon and bought two bottles of water. "For next year," he told me, and dropped them into my bag.

"Who's driving?" I asked.

They all paused nervously.

"Don't look at me," I said. "I drove the whole way here."

Our laughter started as a peep and became thunderous. The three of them happily decided they'd share shifts on the way home.

Three hundred and sixty miles with Gina, Gray, or Max

at the wheel was much quicker than one mile with me. Every time we stopped, we rotated seats. Shotgun controlled the radio, and whoever sat there kept us on a steady diet of hard rock and easy listening. We had musical whiplash by the time the radio died. After that, we told stories.

We laughed harder than I thought was possible. We cried some, too.

The tears led to talk of autumn and the future. Gray was headed down the road to Valparaiso for his freshman year; Gina, Max, and I had two more semesters at Coast Memorial. Bells and teachers and crowds weren't so bad.

With friends.

About halfway home, I texted Mom.

Me: **The Social Experiments worked.**

Her: **You better not be driving and texting.**

Me: **Not a chance.**

Her: **Be safe. I want to hear all about it.**

I had plenty to tell.

Back at the yard, Metal Pete was still up and working in the garage. He slid out from under a Honda Civic and yelled, "So did you find the fountain?"

"Yeah, it was under a big sign that said 'Fountain of Youth,'" I answered.

Metal Pete grinned. "Go figure."

I gathered up my bag from the truck, ran the keys back to him, and scrubbed Headlight between the ears.

"You'll tell me about it?" Metal Pete asked.

"Tomorrow, when I come to work."

"Work?" he asked.

"I sort of need a job if I'm going to start driving again. Gas and insurance and stuff."

He wiped a smudge of grease on my nose. "Does this mean I have to pay you real money?"

"Well, you can't pay me in doughnuts," I said with a laugh.

"Then I suppose I'll see you tomorrow," he said.

When I got back to the group, we stood around as if we weren't sure if the day was over or not.

"Thanks for going with me," I told them.

Gina said, "We should try to road-trip somewhere every anniversary."

We all agreed, but I wasn't sure we'd follow through. Maybe we would.

Gina and Gray walked wearily toward her car, and I asked Max if he'd escort me to the Yaris. Max gave me a little chin-nod, and we trudged toward an aisle I'd been down many times.

"What are we doing?" he asked.

"You'll see."

He didn't seem to need more than that.

Halfway down the Yaris's aisle, we passed the Buick I'd written my list on the first day I brought Max to see Trent's car. Wind had blown the dust around, but it hadn't rained, so the list was still visible. Max ran his hand over the hood, erasing the list, since it was nearly complete. We followed the moonlight to Trent's car.

"What are we doing?" Max asked.

"We're leaving the rest of the past in the past," I told him.

When we reached the Yaris, I asked Max if he needed a moment, but he said no. The old heap didn't draw blood or tears from him as it had the last two times. Instead, Max walked around to the bumper and ripped away the top layer of an *I Love Climbing* sticker.

"I never asked where he got that," I said.

"Souvenir shop in Denver. On family vacation. Right before the accident."

"Did y'all climb?"

Max shook his head. "We tried. He was scared of heights so he bought a sticker and said he'd do it next time."

"Sounds like him," I said.

Trent, lover of star and sky. Fear couldn't tie him to the ground anymore. I think Max and I were both considering that as he let the sticker curl in on itself and placed it in his pocket. Max was taking something with him. I was leaving something behind.

I removed Big from my bag. Empty, he wore only his own gouging scar from where I'd removed his paper stuffing.

The idea had come to me on the drive home from Willit Hill this morning. If the stuffing went into the ground, then Big should go down with the ship—er, Yaris. If I wanted to live in the present, I needed to commit to it. These were tangible choices—an anchor, a trail marker, an emotional tattoo—to recognize the decision.

I opened the Yaris door, set Big in the shotgun seat, and buckled him in.

"You're giving him up?" Max asked.

"He's the old me."

"He's empty."

"Exactly. The new me is full."

Well, hopefully.

I closed the door. The metal-on-metal thud echoed through the yard. From her bed on the porch, Headlight bellowed.

Good-byes are never easy; not even for dogs and stuffed ostriches.

The words and thoughts I'd given to Big over the years, I would give to Max. Or my friends. And my family. That seemed right, and Big wouldn't care. He was just an arcade toy with a hole in his belly.

He was a time machine.

I didn't need him anymore.

"I like it, Kingston," Max said, a long yawn stretching his mouth wide. "I think you're going to be okay."

"Well, I drank from the Fountain of Youth in a Dixie cup, so it's only logical that—"

Max touched my cheek, touched the scar at my mouth, and stopped me from saying anything else. "That one have a name?" he asked.

"The scar? Nope."

He kissed me again. "I'm thinking Max is a pretty solid name."

"Oh, you do, do you?" I asked playfully.

"Well"—*kiss*—"I plan to spend"—*kiss*—"a bunch of"—*kiss*—"time"—*kiss*—"right here." He threw both of our hats on the ground so nothing was in the way. When our lips were tissue-paper-width apart, he said, "That scar's my favorite."

He kissed it again.

I felt the kiss in my eyelashes.

Felt happiness.

If there was such a thing greater than happiness, I felt that, too. Peace, perhaps. Yes, I was definitely more at peace with the Sadie I was now—bangs and scars and T-shirts and forty-five-miles-an-hour driving. Not because Max kissed me or accepted me, or because I worked through my list, or because Gray hijacked my thoughts from Big, but because I wasn't scared of my story anymore.

Sometimes the journey to let someone love you is the journey to loving yourself. I still had plenty more miles to go, but I had Pink Floyd, Tennessee, Idaho, and Max for company.

I had a feeling we'd get along just fine from here.

ACKNOWLEDGMENTS

To God, who knows exactly how much I have in common with Sadie May Kingston. You love me when I'm stuck, when I'm scared, and when I isolate myself. You see my scars and my shame and you still say I am beautiful and redemptive. While I don't always understand, I am so very grateful. Thank you for making art with me.

To Rosemary Brosnan, who also knows how much I have in common with Sadie Kingston. You held my hand in this project and during two very difficult years of life. If you asked for the ends of the earth, I would start walking now. (Well, after I asked you to point in that direction.) You are deeply loved.

To the entire team at Harper: Susan Katz, Kate Jackson, Annie Berger, Bethany Reis, Brenna Franzitta, Erin Fitzsimmons, Heather Daugherty, Kim VandeWater, Aubry

Parks-Fried, Margot Wood, Kathleen Morandini, Patty Rosati, Olivia Russo, Andrea Pappenheimer and the sales team, and all the people who work behind the scenes to make great books.

Kelly Sonnack: Once upon a time this book started in a culinary cooking class, and two thousand pages later . . . it is about salvaging the wreckage of life and the power of truth. That is the odd journey we travel. I'm so thankful I never have to travel alone.

Before I get into my deep thanking lists, I should say this project had three huge turning points: 1. Batcave. 2. Patricia Riley. 3. David Arnold. I can safely say that I owe my sanity and finishing this project to all three. You impacted my work and my heart; I owe you. My mom isn't a turning point, but she reads, edits, and encourages me tirelessly. I wouldn't be here (or anywhere) without her.

To my accountability group and dear friends: C. J. Schooler; Katie, Matt, and Sam Corbin; Leah Spurlin; Brooke Buckley; Alina Klein; and Victoria Schwab.

To my critique partners: Kristin O'Donnell Tubb, Rae Ann Parker, Ruta Sepetys, David Arnold, Erica Rodgers, Lauren Thoman, Patricia Nesbitt, and Janice Erbach.

To my community: Sarah Brown, Paige Crutcher, Ashley and Sherra Schwartau, Dawn Wyant, Myra McEntire, S. R. Johannes, Jennifer Jabaley, Becky Abertalli, Ally Watkins, Kate Dopirak, Sharon Cameron, Jessica Young, Michael Smith, J. W. Scott, Linda and Kent Schwab, everyone at Batcave, the Lucky Fourteeners retreat group, Parnassus Books, Kim Liggett,

Christa Desir, Jolene Perry, Julie Stokes, the wonderful people in the SCBWI Midsouth (What a group!), and my SCBWI LA conference friends from around the country and world.

To my LWC students; Crosspoint Church, Percy Warner Park, State Street UMC; Climb Nashville; Fort Walton Beach, Florida; Daniel Hilton of Sunset Beach Service; and Ballard County.

To teachers, librarians, media specialists, booksellers, bloggers, reviewers, podcasters, and fellow authors.

To Adam. Be the crash. Rhinos forever. Broadway is yours for the taking.

To my family: Mom, Dad, Matt, Angela, Bryce, Brooklyn, Grandmother, Nana, Barbara, Mike, Dave, Sheridon, Taylor, Daniel, Destin, Kristen, Claiborne, Shelby, Kurtis, Matt, and Pat. I love you. Thank you for loving me.

As always, to all you readers. Of the two of us, you will always be my better half.

TURN THE PAGE FOR A LOOK AT
COURTNEY C. STEVENS'S
Faking Normal, OUT NOW.

chapter 1

BLACK funeral dress. Black heels. Black headband in my hair. Death has a style all its own. I'm glad I don't have to wear it very often.

My dress, which I found after rummaging in the back of my closet, still smells vaguely of summer and chlorine. The smell is probably just a memory.

"Alexi, slide in closer so Craig can sit with Kayla." My mother's voice pulls me from my misery and back to the funeral.

Mom makes room for me to shift down the pew toward her, and I slide obediently into the crook of her arm as Kayla's boyfriend joins our family. Even though I don't tell Mom, it feels good when her arm loops over my shoulder, and her hand gives me a little squeeze-pat that means she loves me. If we weren't at a funeral, I'd probably shrug her off. But that would be sort of selfish, since Mrs. Lennox was in Mom's prayer group all that time.

"How's Bodee doing?" Mom asks.

"I don't really know him," I answer.

"You've been in school together for eleven years."

I shrug. "He's the Kool-Aid Kid." Why do adults always think kids should be friends just because their mothers are? Sharing homeroom and next-door lockers doesn't mean you know a person beyond his label. Across the church aisle from me is Rachel Tate, the girl whose mom did Principal James on Bus 32. I'm Kayla Littrell's carbon-copy little sister. Before this week, Bodee was the Kool-Aid Kid. Now, he'll be the kid whose dad murdered his mom. That label will pass from ear to ear whenever Bodee walks down the hall. But now it's a pity-whisper instead of a spite-whisper.

"It would be nice if you reached out to him." I can tell Mom wants to say more, but the music changes and she faces the front.

There are no words to the music, and that makes me sad. Every song deserves lyrics. Deserves a story to tell. Mrs. Lennox's story is over, so maybe she doesn't need words, but Bodee might. Reaching out to him is one of those Christian things my mom talks about, but you can't share a closet and a stack of old football cards with someone you hardly know. So I say a prayer and hope he'll find a place of his own to hide.

But this'll probably always be what he goes back to. Mom. No Mom.

That's a forever change. I never understood life could be so dramatically sectioned, but it can. And is. There is only after. And before.

My moment was by the pool; Bodee's is by the casket. Or wherever he was when he found out about his mom.

Kayla leans away from Craig and asks, "Alexi, is he in your grade?"

I nod and wish Kayla would lower her voice.

"Lord, he's homely," she adds.

"His mom's dead," I say. I inch even closer to Mom, which isn't exactly possible. Kayla's wrong, anyway. He's not homely; he's unkempt, and there's a difference.

I'd rather sit with Liz and Heather, but all the parents have their kids clumped around them like they're trying to share one umbrella in a rainstorm. I love my family, but it seems that I'm always with people I don't know how to talk to when I feel the saddest. With Kayla, and Craig, her appendage. Or Dad, and Mom the teacher.

"Who does he run around with?" Kayla persists.

"No one."

Mom gives Kayla the eye, and we both stare at our programs.

I repeat Psalm 23 with the rest of the crowd and wonder if God ever considered writing the psalm in the past tense, since so many ministers read it during funerals. "Yea, though I walked through the valley of the shadow of death" is more accurate for Mrs. Lennox.

"And now," the pastor says, "we're going to hear from Jean's two sons, Ben and Bodee."

Ben strides forward, never looking up. He removes a piece of paper from his pocket. The room is quiet, and I can hear the page crinkle as he flattens it against the podium. He twists his sealed lips this way and that, and then opens his mouth and sings—half reading, half crying—part of a hymn. The song is beautiful, and I wonder if music is the real language of grief.

"Mom always sang that when she worked in the kitchen." Ben stares at the ceiling as he says, "I don't know how to make it without you, Mom."

His pain and fear pass through the air like electricity. I don't know how they're going to make it either.

"Thank you, Ben," the pastor says. "Bodee, come on up here, son."

All eyes look to the left, where Bodee rises from his seat in the family section.

Bodee's hair is blond today. I'd thought his Kool-Aid-colored locks were intended to disguise his misfit jeans and generic white T-shirts. Make him look artistic instead of just poor, but now I'm not so sure.

Mom moves her arm from my shoulder to crumple a tissue in her hand and dab at her tears. "Oh, this is just awful."

I can't take my eyes off Bodee. His shoulders bend like

the wire hanger in my closet that sags under the weight of my winter coat. I want to put my hand in the center of his back, force him upright. His sluggish shuffle is as sad as his shoulders.

"I think he's wearing Craig's old khakis," Kayla says. "See the faded ring on the back pocket?"

"Half the guys at Rickman chew," I say. But Kayla's right about Craig's khakis; I've seen those same threads spoon and fork and maybe even tongue around Kayla on our couch.

"Well, they're somebody's khakis." There's sympathy in her voice. "Maybe *you* should take him shopping."

Even though it's the kindest thing Kayla's said, I whisper, "Why don't *you* take him shopping?"

"Maybe I will."

Craig rolls his eyes at me, because he knows as well as I do that the last thing Bodee needs is to become one of Kayla's pet projects.

Now Bodee's at the podium, and Mom's not the only one who needs a tissue. While the room sucks and snorts and wipes, he grips the knot on his tie like it's a lap bar on a roller coaster.

He doesn't look at any of us. The microphone broadcasts his short breaths into the room.

Come on, Bodee. Say something.

But he just breathes and tugs at the tie again with one hand and wedges the other into the pocket of Craig's old pair of pants. I pull at the folds of my dress. Kayla does the same.

Mom squeezes Dad's hand. The rest of the room shifts in their discomfort for Bodee.

"That poor, poor boy," Mom whispers.

Lyrics drift into my head as I watch Bodee drown.

Alone.
Before this crowd.
Alone, in this terrible dream.
Who am I in this visible silence?
Can they hear me scream?

I wonder if Bodee knows that song. Doubtful. I toy with the idea of writing the lyrics on the back of the program. I could drop it in his locker on Monday. But he might take that the wrong way.

My mysterious desk guy wouldn't take it the wrong way, though. He penciled those same lyrics on my desk the first week of school. August 8. Nineteen days after my life changed.

I don't think random lyrics are going to help Bodee.

He's not going to talk.

It's like there's a muzzle over his mouth. A word-thief at work.

Bodee bolts from the podium and out the side door.

"Go," Mom says.

For once our instincts are the same. My knee collides with the hymnal holder on the pew in front of us. The crack announces my movement to the room and effectively ends the silence that Bodee started. Craig steadies me as I climb over him and Kayla.

"Good idea," Craig says as I exit.

I'm not going because Mom told me to or because Craig thinks someone should. I know what it's like to face the silence alone.

Bodee's in the back garden. I'm out of breath when I reach him, which is fine because this is awkward already. All this empathy, or whatever it is, will be gone by the 7:55 bell Monday morning. The school hallway is a war of differences, and Bodee and I have plenty. Accepted; rejected. Shops at the mall; doesn't shop at all. Quiet except with friends; quiet everywhere. But today we have something in common besides last names that start with L.

We've both lost something we're never going to get back.

The little concrete bench wobbles as I add my weight to his. He only glances at me long enough to register who I am. There's no surprise on his face that I have followed him to this outdoor hiding place, nor does he send me an *I want to be alone* look.

Time would speed up if I spoke, but I don't care if time is slow. I do wonder what Liz and Heather think about my scramble from the pew, and if everyone in there believes I'll reemerge with a repaired, talking Bodee.

But I don't tell him to go back inside or that everything will be fine. I just sit beside him and let the inch between my thigh and his remain. He cracks his knuckles compulsively, and I stare at a break in the concrete where a little green weed lives.

When the funeral director finds us, I finally speak. "See you Monday?"

"Yeah."

And that's it. I leave Bodee on the bench. The space between us is elastic now, stretching from an inch into yards.

When I reach my mom, she kisses my forehead. "Lex, I love you," she says.

"I love you, too." And as I say it, I think, No one will say that to Bodee anymore.

JOIN THE

Epic Reads
COMMUNITY

THE ULTIMATE YA DESTINATION ///////////////

◀ **DISCOVER** ▶
your next favorite read

◀ **MEET** ▶
new authors to love

◀ **WIN** ▶
free books

◀ **SHARE** ▶
infographics, playlists, quizzes, and more

◀ **WATCH** ▶
the latest videos

◀ **TUNE IN** ▶
to Tea Time with Team Epic Reads